April 28th, 2001

For Craig –

I hope this is a good book with a intresting story.

Patsy

The LINK BOYS

By Constance Fecher

VENTURE FOR A CROWN

HEIR TO PENDARROW

BRIGHT STAR: *A Portrait of Ellen Terry*

THE LINK BOYS

THE LINK BOYS

CONSTANCE FECHER

Drawings by Richard Cuffari

AN ARIEL BOOK

FARRAR, STRAUS & GIROUX

NEW YORK

First edition, 1971

Library of Congress catalog card number: 75-149219

SBN 374.3.4497.3

Printed in the United States of America

Published simultaneously in Canada by

Doubleday Canada Ltd., Toronto

Designed by Cynthia Krupat

For Raymond

Contents

The LINK BOYS

Chapter 1

The Gold Purse

It was on a morning in May that I saw Joshua for the first time, though then of course I didn't know who he was or even his name and never dreamed of the adventures I was to share with him and his Link Boys.

As a matter of fact, I was in rather low spirits that day for a very good reason, as you will hear, and when we passed the bit of waste ground where the Fleet River runs into the Thames, I stopped and looked longingly at a showman's booth. At the entrance stood a strange little man not more than four feet high, with a beard to his waist and a red pointed hat.

"Walk up, walk up, ladies and gentlemen," he was shouting in a high, squeaky voice. "Here you will see all the wonders of the universe, a mermaid in a barrel, a woman with two heads, wild men from Borneo blacker than coal . . ."

My Uncle Jeremy looked down at my miserable face

and grinned. "Go on," he said. "In with you." And he paid our two pennies and in we went.

There was a rank, musty smell; the mermaid was no more than a sea horse in a bottle, and the two heads nodding at one another were suspiciously like the puppet show at Christmas. But it wasn't all a fraud.

"The biggest animal in the world," the voice was bawling outside, and it was too. Chained to a post, it was enormous, with a hide like black shiny leather and a gigantic horn growing out of its snout. I wasn't afraid. After all, I was twelve years old and very nearly grown up. But I must confess that when the great head with two fierce little pigs' eyes swayed toward me, I did step back right onto my uncle's toes.

"It's a rhinoceros. They come from Africa," he said a trifle put out. "Come on, Tom, you must have seen enough of these ugly freaks by now. I know I have. Let's get out of here."

"Phew! That's better!" went on my uncle as we came out into the fresh air of the street. "It was hot enough in there to suffocate an ox. I began to believe myself back in the jungle."

"Have you been to Africa, then?" I asked curiously. Uncle Jeremy was always coming out with surprising bits of information. I had lived with him for two years now, and I still knew very little about him.

"Yes, once," he replied shortly. "I went on a voyage to make my fortune and came back a great deal poorer than I set out. Now tidy yourself, boy, for goodness' sake. We don't want Master Fox to think you one of these idle ragamuffins with nothing better to do than gape at every peep show."

"Yes, Uncle," I said hastily and sighed. Paying a penny

to look at the rhinoceros had been only the sugar on a very nasty pill. We were on our way to speak with Master Fox, who ran a successful drapery business. Provided he liked the look of me, I would be apprenticed to him for seven long years, and I was not looking forward to it one little bit.

For one thing, his shop had a peculiar dry smell from the rolls of woolens, velvets, and silks. For another, I didn't at all fancy standing outside in the street in all weathers from six in the morning till nine at night bawling "What d'ye lack?" until I was hoarse, and trying to attract the attention of the women customers bustling along to market.

I didn't know exactly what I did want to do, but one thing I was sure of. I did want to have some fun, and there didn't seem much promise of that in the prospect before me.

It was only a week since Uncle Jeremy had spoken to me very seriously one evening as we were getting ready to go to bed in the room we shared in Bridewell Court.

"You can't go on like this, my boy," he said, "roaming the streets all day and getting into mischief. You must have a trade, some settled occupation to keep you steady."

"I'm sorry about the apple woman, Uncle," I said very quickly. The boy next door had bet me a halfpenny that I couldn't steal three apples in succession from the stall on the corner, and I would have won it if the man with the barrel of salted herring hadn't pounced on me just as I was making my getaway. "I won't do it again, really I won't."

My uncle grinned at me. "It's not that so much, Tom lad, but you've got to have the chance of making something of yourself. Why, think where you could end up.

Lord Mayor of London, maybe. Sir Thomas Hawke, eh, with a gold chain round your neck and a carriage like Dick Whittington."

As if anyone believed that old fairy tale any longer, I thought scornfully. A boy who came penniless to London Town with a cat, of all things, and made a fortune!

"Look at me," my uncle went on with his peculiar lop-sided smile. "Here I am at thirty-two, and not worth a brass farthing."

I looked up at him. He was a tall man with a brown face, curling dark hair, smiling blue eyes, and tiny gold rings in his ears like a sailor. I wanted to say that I'd rather be like him than anyone else in the world.

He had come into my life in a very strange way, and if it had not been for him, I wouldn't be telling this tale now. You see, my father and mother had both died in the same week from the great plague sickness when I was only four years old. I don't remember much about that time, only the silent house and myself crying and crying because I was so hungry and my mother lying on the bed and not moving when I shook her.

I remember how dark it grew and the rats that ran across the floor and over my feet. I remember screaming in terror as I ran out of the room and fell headlong down the wooden stairs. I suppose it must have been a long time before they found me, because after that I was ill and can't remember very much, only a muddle of always being cold and hungry.

They took me to the great poorhouse where all the orphaned children had been herded together. I lived there for six years, but time has no meaning when you know only brutality and a loneliness without hope. Then one day I was sitting on the stone floor shredding the hemp that we were kept at all day to earn our keep, when a voice spoke to me, very gentle and quiet.

"Tom," it said, and I looked up very fearful, wondering what I'd done wrong this time.

"It is Tom, isn't it?" he went on. "Tom Hawke?" And it was my Uncle Jeremy. He had come back from a long sea voyage and, finding that my father, who was his brother, had died, had been searching for me everywhere.

It was like being lifted out of hell into heaven. We were not rich. In fact, I still didn't know what he did to earn a living. But he fed and clothed me. He taught me to read and write and, above all, he talked to me as though I were a real person and grown up like himself. I loved him more than anyone in the world. The thought that if Master Fox liked me I would be living in his house from now on and would only see my uncle occasionally was what was making me feel so wretchedly unhappy.

By this time we had walked up from Ludgate and reached Cheapside. Above our heads, rattling and clanking in the wind hung the great shop signs, a scarlet lion, a golden eagle, a sheep, a flying horse, and three silver lilies. Outside the tavern, on the corner of Milk Street, two men were hauling up a splendid picture of his blessed Majesty, King Charles II, with long, glossy curls and black mustachios. Twelve years ago he had been restored to the throne of his father, the Martyr King Charles I, whose head had been barbarously chopped off long before I was born.

We were just about to cross the road and turn down Lombard Street when it happened. A coach painted scarlet and green with a gilt coat of arms on the door and pulled by six splendid horses came thundering down the center of the road. It swerved to avoid a market cart loaded with carcasses, swayed dangerously, then crashed into one of the posts set up to protect pedestrians. There was a grinding crack as the axletree smashed and the coach came to a lurching halt.

A crowd gathered in an instant, with my uncle and me wedged in the middle of it. The coachman jumped down from his box and abused the carter, who swore back at him among his tumbled sides of beef and mutton. The two footmen leaped from their perch at the back of the carriage and began shouting in turn.

Then as the gilded door swung open, everyone fell silent and the finest gentleman I had ever set eyes on stepped out of the coach. He wore a purple velvet coat embroidered with gold, fine lace with winking diamonds at his throat, beribboned breeches, and a hat with sweeping white feathers. To cap it all, he was in an absolutely tearing rage. He stormed at the coachman, the carter, the footmen, with a flow of language I never expected from so great a lord. Then quite suddenly he clapped his hand to his pocket and his voice rose into a scream of fury.

"My purse! It has gone . . . this very moment. I felt the robber's hand as he thrust against me. Demme, there he goes! Stop that boy! Stop, thief!"

It all happened in a flash. Someone seemed to press against me, something cold and hard was pushed into my hands. Automatically my fingers closed around it. Then a boy, taller and older than myself, ragged and dirty, with wild dark hair, was shouting and pointing.

"That's him! That's the cutpurse! There he is! Look, master!"

The crowd fell back a little and I was alone, separated from my uncle, facing the furious owner of the coach.

In my hands I held a purple velvet purse, the gold clasp studded with small gems that sparkled in the sunshine.

"But I didn't," I stammered like any great fool. "I didn't steal it . . . really I didn't . . . I don't know where it came from . . . I . . ."

"Just flew into your hands, did it?" sneered the fine gentleman. "You sneaking pickpocket! You lying rascal! Call the constable, one of you!"

The cry was quickly taken up, and eager bystanders hurried away to do his bidding.

Uncle Jeremy had thrust his way through to my side. He said firmly, "You are mistaken, sir. This is some trick. My nephew has never stolen so much as a farthing in his life. I can swear to that."

"Indeed, and who may you be?" asked the gentleman haughtily.

"Who I am is of little importance." My uncle took the purse from my hands and returned it to its owner with a slight bow. "Your property, sir, returned intact and no harm done."

There was a moment's pause. The fine gentleman was staring at him and it was strange but I could have sworn there was a glint of recognition in the narrowed eyes.

"Oh no," he went on at last. "Not so fast, my man. Don't think you'll escape me so easily. I know your sort. A smooth-tongued rogue if ever I saw one. You stole it yourself no doubt, then slipped it to this young whipper-snapper, hoping to escape the law by putting the blame on the boy. Where are the guineas that filled the purse, eh? Answer me that!" And triumphantly he turned the velvet bag upside down, showing it flat and empty. He

waved a beringed hand to his two footmen. "Ben, Will! Seize this fellow. Hold him firm till the constable comes. I'll take him before a magistrate and charge him myself if it's the last thing I do."

Out of the corner of his mouth Uncle Jeremy whispered, "Run, Tom, run quickly, as fast as you can. Don't worry about me. I'll get out of this somehow."

I didn't want to leave him, but he pushed me away and then put up a great show of resistance when the two footmen grasped him by the arms. I saw him knock one of them down and then tackle the other, and under cover of the shouting and confusion, I dived through the crowd, tearing myself away from clutching hands.

I raced down Cheapside, dodged across the road, skirted around the back of St. Paul's Cathedral, and pulled up breathless on the other side. I leaned against the edge of a flat tombstone, still panting and so bewildered by the sudden turn of events that for a moment I could hardly take in what had happened.

All around me lay the charred and blackened ruins of the great cathedral destroyed in the fire which had raged through the city only six years before. A few feet away from me, a bony pig rooted in the grimy ashes and a wild mangy cat shot out and tore across my feet.

I was just trying to make up my mind what I should do when a voice behind me spoke jeeringly.

"Well, you're a green one and no mistake! Standing there with a look on your face like one of the loonies out of the madhouse!"

I swung around. At a little distance stood the boy who had accused me, his legs apart, his hands in the pockets of his ragged coat, a mocking grin on the dark face.

"It was you!" I exclaimed. "It was you who stole the purse!"

"Right first time, and fine pickings they were too." And the boy impudently pulled a hand from his pocket, tossed a gold piece in the air, and caught it again. "Ten little golden Jimmy-Goblins, and every one of them spanking-new guineas from the Mint."

"But that's stealing," I burst out indignantly. "And you tried to put the blame on me."

"Had to do something or they'd have nabbed me." The boy looked me up and down with a certain scorn. "Any-one with the sense they were born with would have drop-ped it into his pocket, not stood staring like a stupid ninny fallen out of the moon."

"I'm not a thief," I shouted back at him furiously, "and it was all your fault. Now they've accused my uncle and I don't know what will happen."

"I can tell you that." The boy fixed me with his piercing dark eyes and spoke with a slow relish. "If it had been you, they'd have let you off with a whipping, but as for him—well, if he gets old Beaky, the hanging judge, when he's brought to trial, then he'll swing for it, sure as the sun rises."

A cold shudder ran right through me. "Hang? But he's done nothing."

"What does that matter?" mocked the boy. "Up he'll go by the neck until . . . c-r-r-rrack! He's dead!" And gri-macing horribly, he jerked his head to one side, his tongue lolling out. He sidestepped quickly as I made a rush at him, and shot out a foot, neatly tripping me up, so that I sprawled in the filthy gray dust. By the time I had scram-bled to my feet, he had gone.

I stood for a moment, horrified at what he had said. In an odd way, his audacity fascinated and repelled me at the same time. But how could I leave my uncle to such a terrible fate? I had to find out exactly what had happened. I had to try to save him. I squared my shoulders and set out resolutely for our lodging.

Chapter 2

I Escape a Great Danger

Bad news travels quickly, and everyone was talking about it by the time I reached Bridewell Court. The neighbors were standing at the doors of the houses, staring at me as I came through the gateway. We had always kept to ourselves, my uncle and I, we'd not made many friends, and now the neighbors were all only too eager to point a spiteful finger at us.

"Caught out at last, are ye?" called one.

"Master Jeremy'll not keep his nose stuck up so high in Newgate," jeered another.

"Save when he swings up aloft at Tyburn," grinned the third.

"What did ye do with the swag, eh, Tommy m'lad," a hoarse voice whispered, and a rough black beard was thrust against my cheek.

I swung myself free from him and went on down the

road. I longed to shout back at them, to tell them it was all a mistake, that my uncle had done nothing, but I knew if I did, they'd all be on me like a pack of dogs. So I walked through them with my head held high till I reached the doorway of our lodging. Mistress Larkin pounced on me at once.

"Oh, Tommy, what a dreadful calamity, to be sure! Your dear uncle taken up like a common thief and you left all alone, poor precious lamb, with no one but me to care what becomes of you!"

She put her arms around me and I fought myself free. I'd always hated her. She was our landlady, a stout woman with fat cheeks round and rosy as apples. She was a washerwoman by trade. All about her hung the sour smell of the great tubs of soapy water forever boiling in the yard. She was always hanging around my uncle and pretending to make much of me, calling me "lovey-dovey," and "little orphaned lambkin," and other idiotic names as if I were a baby. But she had little black eyes, hard and shiny as buttons, and Jenny, her maid, who slaved all day over the buckets of water, was often black and blue from the kicks and pinches freely given her by her mistress.

I broke away from her and went up to our attic room under the rafters. The moment I entered it, I knew she'd been there before me. Uncle Jeremy was very neat. Everything had to be kept in its place.

"It's the only way on board ship, Tom," he said to me once, "when you've got scarce a foot or so to call your own and your mate's shakedown is a bare six inches away from you."

It was not that the room was untidy, but I was certain she had been there, poking her nose into our few possessions, and it made my blood boil. I ran across to the truckle bed and dragged it away from the wall, but thank goodness the box was safe.

My uncle kept his money in a very secret place. As I said, we weren't rich, but sometimes he had come home with a handful of gold pieces. He would put one on the table with a smile. "That's for you and me, Tom lad. We'll be off and enjoy ourselves, eh?" And we would too. The fair at Southwark with money to spend on all the sideshows, or Sadlers Wells out at Islington with country dancing and a grand supper of roasted duckling and green peas with sweet creamy sillabubs and a sip of Canary to drink the King's health.

The rest of the gold would go into the black box. "That's to set you up as a fine gentleman one of these days, Tom." And he cut a square hole in the floorboards, slipped in the box, and fitted the wood back so as you'd never know. Then we pulled the bed over it, just to make sure. "Safe as the Tower of London," said my uncle with a grin.

And it was safe still. Mistress Larkin's black button eyes weren't as sharp as she thought they were.

After I had pushed back the bed, I sat on the edge of it, feeling even more miserable than in those dreadful days in the poorhouse, because then I'd never known what it was like to live with Uncle Jeremy.

Jenny called up the stairs that I could go down to supper with them, but I felt as if even a crumb of bread would have choked me, so I stayed where I was. It was hot under the roof, and presently I crossed to the window and pushed the casement wide open.

It was high enough up so you could see right down the river to London Bridge. I used to love to watch the gulls swooping down to the mud at the water's edge and hear their sharp, screaming cry. There were always boats going up and down, and sometimes the barges of great noblemen, all gold and scarlet and blue, musicians playing on the poop and boys singing. But tonight I wouldn't have been interested if it had been the King himself going by. An idea had suddenly come to me. If I took all the money in the black box and gave it to the grand gentleman who had been robbed, perhaps he would let my uncle go free. Then my heart sank. I had no idea who he was or how I could reach him, and would he listen to me even if I did? I was puzzling over my problem when I heard voices. It was Mistress Larkin and someone I didn't know and they were talking of my uncle. They must have been in the room below, with the window open, for the sound was quite clear.

"I never trusted him, never," said the landlady. "Coming in one day with a fistful of gold pieces and the next without a farthing to bless himself with. It isn't natural."

"Aye, you're right there," agreed the other voice. "One of these light-fingered gentlemen, no doubt, picking pockets and worse, I shouldn't wonder. A murderer too, unless he's lucky! He'd half killed that poor footman and had started on the other before ever I came up."

I went hot with rage to hear such wicked lies, but the next moment was even worse.

"Wasn't there a boy with him?" went on the stranger.

"That there was, Master Constable," replied Mistress Larkin in what I called her creepy-crawly voice. "He's upstairs now, a fine sturdy lad, and all alone in the world. No kith nor kin save this uncle of his."

"Is that so? Well, I'll be right glad to lay my hands on him and that's a fact. Proper cursing I got for letting him get away, as if I've got a dozen hands and eyes for every rascal!"

"Will they put him into Newgate?" asked Mistress Larkin.

"Not if they can help it," answered the constable sourly. "Not much to be got out of a young varmint like that. It'll be a thrashing for him, and the house of correction. There's plenty of work for such as he if his uncle swings at Tyburn. Charity children come cheap, a bite of food and no wages. There's many as'll be only too glad to take him off the Parish."

"I could do with a boy like that," went on Mistress Larkin. "That lazy slut of a maid is always grumbling that she finds the tubs too heavy to lift. He could earn his keep twice over in the scullery and the washhouse. A word in the right place, Master Constable, and there could be a little something for you too."

"Well, mistress . . . as a favor to you. I tell you what. You keep him locked up safe and sound till morning, then I'll see what I can do."

"Ah, you're a good man, and a kindhearted one, Master Constable." I could imagine the fat smile of satisfaction on Mistress Larkin's face. "You'll take a drink of ale before you go." And they laughed together, pleased at the cheap bargain fixed between them.

I shivered at the thought of what they could do to me. It would either be back to all the horror of the poorhouse or else I'd be like Jenny, dependent on Mistress Larkin for every morsel of food, with nothing to look forward to but hard knocks and the skin off my back if I didn't do just as she commanded.

It was then that everything my Uncle Jeremy had taught me came crowding into my mind. I wouldn't wait

for others to tell me what to do. I would strike out for myself.

I would escape. I would run away now, this very night, before they realized that I knew anything of what they intended. Where I would go and how I would live, I hadn't the faintest notion. My one idea was to get out of the house and as far away as possible.

Once I had made up my mind, I began to make a bundle of our few possessions. Both my uncle and I had been wearing our best clothes for the interview with Master Fox—how far away all that seemed now! It was difficult to believe it had only been that morning that I was dreading it so much!

Anyway, I found our spare clean shirts and one or two other articles of clothing, and then I looked at the seaman's chest beside my uncle's bed. It was far too heavy to take with me, and yet it was so much part of him that I hesitated before opening it. I lifted the lid only because there might be things in it that he valued which I wouldn't want to leave behind.

On the top lay his lute. He used to strum it sometimes on a winter evening. He had taught me to sing a little, old ballads and songs of the sea. By pure chance I had a quick ear for the right note and I learned very easily. Sometimes we had all the neighbors joining in. I hummed the lines under my breath.

> "*On Friday morn as we set sail,*
> *It was not far from land,*
> *O there I spy'd a fair pretty maid*
> *With a comb and glass in her hand.*
> *The stormy winds did blow*
> *And the raging seas did roar . . .*"

I couldn't go on. It reminded me of him too keenly. I put the lute on one side. Underneath there was a coat, rather worn and stained, some neckcloths and an old pair of boots, several books and, right at the bottom, something wrapped carefully in an old handkerchief.

When I took it out, it fell open and there in my hands lay a woman's glove, the white silk gone yellow with age, the gold embroidery tarnished, yet still with a faint sweet perfume clinging to it.

I stared at it stupefied. It seemed such a strange thing for my uncle to treasure. I had never thought of a woman in his life. He never spoke of wife or sweetheart. Yet he must have kept this for years, all through his voyages and goodness knows what adventures.

Somehow I couldn't bear to leave it for Mistress Larkin's curious eyes. I wrapped it up again and put it with the lute in my bundle.

In the end my escape was rather hurried. I heard a sound of voices and a great deal of commotion down below. Leaning out of my window, I saw Mistress Larkin come out, followed by Jenny, who staggered under the weight of an enormous laundry basket. They marched down Bridewell Court like a ship in full sail with a small tug bobbing behind. No doubt a customer had sent an urgent request for his clean linen. Now was my opportunity.

I quickly knotted my bundle together, slid down the stairs, and went out the back door. Then I climbed the low wall and made my way down to the waterside. I knew where I could find shelter for one night at least.

Walt Budge, the boatman, was an old friend of mine ever since the day he saved me from drowning. I used to love to take off my shoes and stockings and splash through the cool mud into the river, and one hot day last summer I ventured out too far. The wash from a big boat going downstream swept me off my feet, and under I went. It was Walt who hauled me out, spanked my bottom, just to "teach me a lesson" he said, then gave me an apple and offered to teach me to swim.

After that I had many a trip across river in his wherry, and I knew that at night he hauled it into a ramshackle shed built high up on the bank. It would be a wonderful hiding place till morning when I could think again. It was not until I had climbed into the *Saucy Lady* and settled myself comfortably on the cushions he kept for his more fashionable passengers that I remembered. I had left in such a hurry that I had forgotten Uncle Jeremy's black box under the floorboards.

There was no help for it. I simply had to go back. For one thing, little though it was, it was all the money we had in the world, and for another, I just didn't want Mistress Larkin to have it. Perhaps if I went at once, I could get in and out again before she returned.

Luck favored me at first. I left my bundle stowed in the boat and raced back across the mud and over the wall again. All was still quiet. I had just reached the attic and was dragging the bed away from the wall when I heard Mistress Larkin's sharp voice. The door slammed downstairs and I knew that I was lost.

Now I should have to wait until everyone was asleep, and then of course the doors would be locked and barred. Even the one into the backyard had three bolts, and as I knew very well, they were rusted and very stiff.

It was already dark, but I didn't want to attract attention by lighting my candle, so I sat on the edge of the bed, nursing the box, waiting and waiting. Twice the watchman outside cried the hour. Then for the third time I heard his heavy tread and his staff tapping at the doors as he went by.

"Take heed to your clock: beware your lock, your fire, and your light and God give you good night. One o'clock."

I listened and the house seemed very silent. I opened the door cautiously and stole down the wooden staircase. To my ears each tread creaked and cracked as though a charging army were thundering down. I paused on the landing outside Mistress Larkin's door with my heart in my mouth, but there was no stir. Thankfully I went on.

To reach the topmost bolt I had to fetch a stool from the kitchen. I was balancing on it and wrenching at the iron hasp with all my strength when the bolt suddenly flew back, the stool shot from under my feet, and I went crashing to the floor.

Jenny, who slept in a tiny box-like cupboard off the passage, began at once to scream. I scrambled to my feet and called softly through the door to her, "It's me, Tom, don't be frightened." But I suppose she was too terrified to take in what I said, and she went on screaming.

I was still frantically tugging at the other bolts when the door on the landing crashed back and Mistress Larkin herself appeared, looking enormous in her flowing bed gown and white nightcap, with a broom in one hand and a candlestick in the other. She couldn't have recognized me in the flickering light, because she started down the stairs screaming, "Help! Robbers, thieves, murderers! Help!" and began to belabor me with the broom.

Goodness knows what would have happened if the last bolt had not shot back. Somehow I got the door open and tore across the yard, with her still screeching and stumbling after me. Windows and doors burst open in the other houses, lights flickered and people shouted to one another.

It was a dark, moonless night and it was that which saved me. I got over the wall, skinning my hands on the rough stone, and by the time the neighbors realized what was happening, I had cut across the gardens, over the mud-banks, and reached the boathouse and safety.

My hands were torn and bleeding, my shoes caked with slimy mud, my shoulders ached with the beating and my lungs felt fit to burst, but all the same I had a sweet feeling of triumph. I had outwitted Mistress Larkin and was free of the constable. Somehow, though I had no idea in what way I could do it, I was going to save my Uncle Jeremy.

Chapter 3

The Plague House

"Come on, out of there, young feller. Shift yourself! Double-quick now!"

I woke up to a hand roughly shaking me by the shoulder and stared into a big round face fringed with bushy red whiskers. For a moment I couldn't think where I was or why I was so stiff and cramped. Then the door of the shed flew back in the wind. I could see the sun sparkling on the river, and everything came rushing back.

"It's me, Tom Hawke," I mumbled, and began to scramble out of the boat.

"I can see that," remarked Walt Budge sharply, lifting out my bundle and dumping it beside me. "And if you've got any such notion as stowing away or running off from your uncle, you'd better put it clean out of your head here and now. You cut right back home this minute before you get his stick across your shoulders."

"You don't understand," I protested breathlessly as he hustled me out of the hut, baggage and all. "He's been arrested. He's in prison."

"He's what?" The waterman stopped dead in his tracks and stared at me. "If this is some tale . . ."

"It isn't, really it isn't. It's true, every word. Please listen. I did think that perhaps you might be able to help."

"Oh, you did, did you? Well, I'm not getting myself mixed up with the law, make very sure of that!" And Walt Budge sat himself on the edge of the boat and unwrapped his breakfast of bread and cheese. I couldn't help it. My mouth watered at the sight of the food, and he looked up at me with a grin.

"Here." He broke off a crust and threw it to me. "Come on now, out with it. I haven't all day. I've a living to earn."

So I told him the whole story, though I didn't say anything about the boy. I don't know why. He was the cause of it all, and yet in spite of this, there had been something attractive in his bold defiance, something gay and wild and impudent that I envied. Anyway, I told myself it was something between him and me and nobody else.

"M-m-m," grunted Walt Budge when I had come to an end. "Well, it's a bad business, I must say. He'll be brought before the magistrate, that's for sure, and he'll have to stand trial. Tell you what, boy, you'd better get yourself into Newgate to see him. Find out the truth of the matter and how the land lies."

"But how can I?" I asked desperately.

"Lord bless my soul! Don't you know anything? If you've got a shilling to grease his palm, the turnkey on the gate will let you in quick as a shot. Don't say who you are, mind. Say you've come from his wife or his sweetheart with a spare shirt and such. And another thing.

Remember this. If you've cash, you can live soft in Newgate, but if not . . ." He grimaced horribly.

"You mean you have to pay to be in prison?" I stared at him aghast.

"Aye, my innocent. Pay and pay, through the nose too. Otherwise it's bread and water and lie on the stone floor as best you can." Walt Budge was looking at me, rubbing his chin thoughtfully. "What I don't like is your running off from your lodging like this. You'd have been better off to have stayed."

"No," I said indignantly. "No, I couldn't. Don't you see? Mistress Larkin would be at me all the time and she'd never let me out of her sight for a second. You don't know what she's like."

"Mebbe I do. I were married once . . . and regretted it." He grinned at me. "Where are you going to live, eh? Have you thought o'that?"

"I'll find somewhere."

"Well," he said consideringly, "you can come back here for tonight, but after that, young Dick'll be back and he sleeps in the boat o'nights when we're working late, and I wouldn't trust him too far if there's any questions asked."

Walt showed me where I could hide my bundle and I sat on one of the bollards to which the boats were moored and watched him row along to the landing steps where all the watermen waited for passengers.

It was a lovely morning. Over the river the sun touched the roofs and spires with gold. The boatmen were calling cheerfully to one another, and one of them was singing, his voice sweet and true in the fresh, cool air.

Down by the water's edge there was a smell of tar and salt, an indescribable tang of boats and river mud that somehow made me dreadfully homesick for Uncle Jeremy. I watched longingly as Walt took up his first fare and the powerful stroke of his oars sent the wherry bouncing forward, shooting the strong currents under London Bridge and making for Deptford.

Then I washed my face and hands in the river, wiped them on my handkerchief, walked up Cock Alley, and made my way toward Newgate.

I had put together my uncle's clean shirt and one or two other necessities into a bundle and taken a few coins from the black box. Now I stood inwardly quaking and stared up at the great gate that spanned the road. It had been burned in the fire and only recently rebuilt. Huge figures had been set up above the arch. On the Holborn side I could see Liberty with Whittington's cat at the foot of the statue, and looking toward Cheapside, there were Justice, Mercy, and Truth. The prison itself looked very black and formidable as I walked trembling up to it.

There were a great many people going in and out, and astonishingly, it all worked out as Walt Budge had said. The man at the door eyed me suspiciously enough, but he ran his eye down a long list of names, then took the silver shilling I handed over, trying it cautiously in his teeth before he nodded his head and let me go through. As the gate clanged behind me, I knew a moment of terror just like that a rabbit must feel when the steel trap falls.

I shuddered as I hurried through Press Yard. This was where the prisoners who refused to plead were pegged out on the rough flagstones and iron weights piled onto their chests until, gasping and choking, they either died or yielded to their torturers. Today it was empty, but when I came into the central court of the prison I stopped, appalled.

It seemed to me that everybody in London must be crowded into this narrow space. The noise was terrific, and the sour stench too. There were painted women in bright silks, old men in rags, ruffians and gentlemen, clergymen and beggars, decent family groups with children, people playing cards, throwing dice, eating, sleeping, squabbling, screaming, fighting. I looked around me in despair. How should I ever find my uncle in this hopeless confusion? They pressed around me, putting out filthy hands to touch my clothes, to snatch at my bundle, gabbling at me so that I wanted to put my hands over my ears and run away.

Then a quiet voice spoke behind me. "Well, Tom, my brave lad, how did you find your way here?" And there was Uncle Jeremy, smiling, neat as always, even in this horrible place. My heart gave a great lurch and it was all I could do not to throw my arms around his neck and burst into tears. He put a hand on my shoulder and led me away to a comparatively quiet corner.

"You didn't say who you were?" he asked anxiously. "When they brought me before the magistrate yesterday, there were questions asked about you."

I shook my head and pushed the bundle into his hands. "I said I was bringing you clean linen."

I looked about at all the poor wretches surrounding us and shuddered. "Uncle, Walt Budge said that if I brought you money, you could have a room to yourself, comfort and good food . . ."

"No." He smiled down at me. "I've been in worse places than this. The lower deck of a ship can be a pretty good hell, you know. You get used to it. And those few guineas in the box are all there'll be for you if the worst should happen."

I couldn't bear to hear him say it. "They can't hang you for something you haven't done. They can't."

"Well, we shall see," he said calmly. "It'll be a fortnight at least, if not longer, before I come up for trial and learn my fate. A great deal may happen in that time." He paused and looked away from me before he went on reluctantly. "I fear we've made a powerful enemy, Tom boy."

"The fine gentleman?" I breathed. "You know who he is?"

"Yes, I do. It is my Lord Maltravers," said my uncle with his wry twisted smile. "Close bosom friend of the King and once upon a time my old master."

I gaped at him, I was so surprised. "How? When? You never told me."

"It was a very long time ago and we parted on bad terms," he replied. "I didn't think he recognized me, great man as he has become, but I was mistaken. He'd not forgotten. Otherwise, I'd not be here now."

"Forgotten what?"

But my uncle didn't answer. He took a quick look around and moved closer. "Tom, there is something you can do for me. Something which may save me if I'm lucky."

"What is it?"

"During this past year I have done occasional work for the Navy Office. I want you to carry a letter to Master Pepys at his house in Seething Lane near to the Tower of London. If he would speak for me, it might help my case. Do you think you can do that?"

"Of course."

"Good lad."

"Shall I take it now?"

"Yes. I wrote it out, just in case. Put it safe in your pocket and then don't come here again. It's no place for you. I'll get word to Mistress Larkin somehow."

"But I'm not . . ." I began and then stopped. I'd never in my life lied to my uncle, but to tell him that I'd run away would only add another anxiety. I was on my own now. I must look after myself and him too. So I bit back the words. Instead I said, "I'd rather come, really I would. You see, it's going to be lonely on my own. I shall miss you dreadfully."

He patted my cheek. "We've had some good times, Tommy, and we'll have some more," he said cheerfully. "Now go, and don't forget Master Pepys. It could be important."

"I'll go now," I promised.

The Navy Office was a tall building in a narrow lane. It frowned down at me forbiddingly and the clerk in the outer office looked me up and down disdainfully when I arrived, hot, breathless, and covered with dust. I don't know why I'd run all the way from Newgate, except that I was sure the sooner the message was delivered, the better.

He was a very young man but he put on a great many fine airs. He was sitting behind a tall desk with a huge quill pen in his hand and an open ledger before him.

"Master Pepys," I stammered out. "I must see Master Pepys."

"Must you, now? H'indeed!" he said in a lofty manner. "Well, Master Pepys ain't here. He's away down at His Majesty's dockyards at . . ."

"Then I'll go there," I exclaimed impetuously and prepared to dash out again.

"At His Majesty's dockyards at Portsmouth," he went on, raising his voice and grinning maliciously.

I stopped halfway through the door. You see, all the way there I had pictured myself pleading passionately for my uncle, going down on my knees if needs be—but Portsmouth! It might as well have been on the moon, for all the good it was to me. I said lamely, "I carry a letter for him. Would you see he has it the moment he returns? It is very important."

"You don't say! Some begging petition or other, I'll be bound. Very well. Hand it over."

I had a fierce desire to kick him hard on the shins, to shout at him, to make him realize that it was a matter of life and death, but I knew it wouldn't do any good. Already he was bent over his ledger again. I opened my mouth and shut it again. Then I turned on my heel and went out.

Henry says that what happened afterward that day must have been the workings of fate, because one thing led to another as if by mere chance and yet it all made a pattern. But then Henry and her mother are theater folk and they always believe in luck and good fortune and all kinds of superstitious things such as not whistling in the dressing room and never repeating the last line of a play and hanging charms and amulets over their make-up mirrors. But I'm forgetting. You don't know yet who Henry is. I'm running on too fast. I must tell it all in order just as it fell out.

It was a long walk back to the waterside where Walt Budge kept his boat, and it was late afternoon by the time I reached Blackfriars. I was so deep in thought about where I could find some kind of a lodging out of Mistress Larkin's reach that I walked clean past Cock Alley and was almost at the Temple Gate before I realized where I was.

I turned down Salisbury Court, which is a short cut to the river, and as I passed the Dorset Garden Theatre, the doorkeeper shot out of his box and grabbed me by the arm.

"Here, boy, run to the Three Tuns. Bring me back a can of ale and there's a penny for you. Quick now, or Master Betterton will be roaring his head off. Dry as a bone he says he is . . ."

Master Thomas Betterton was the leading actor, and no doubt he had just come off thirsty and sweating after one of his scenes and his dresser had forgotten his customary draught. I raced to the tavern and back again. The doorkeeper was waiting. Thankfully, he snatched the tankard out of my hand and left a coin in my palm. I stared at it for a moment before I went on my way. It had given me a splendid idea.

The Dorset Garden Theatre had only just been built and was very fine indeed. The Duke of York's Company of actors played there and it was always crowded. They were said to be doing better than even the King's Men in Drury Lane, though Uncle Jeremy had shaken his head when once I begged if we could see a play. Of course it did cost a lot of money; a shilling, even in the topmost gallery; you could feed a family for a whole day for that.

But the idea that had occurred to me was this. There were always odd jobs to be done when the audiences were thronging in and out. Rich patrons would pay you a penny or two to keep their place for them in the queue waiting to go in. There were horses to hold or errands to be run. The actors were forever sending out for food and drink and they were lavish with their tips. It was a wonderful notion. If I showed myself willing, I felt sure I would be able to keep myself without touching the precious contents of the black box.

Well, that was the first link in the chain of coincidence. The next one was not so pleasant. I had bought myself a meat pasty from the cookshop on the corner and I sat down on the steps at the back of the theater overlooking the river.

I had eaten it to the last crumb and was just wishing I had another when I heard the sharp whining yelps of an animal in pain. There was a girl's voice, high-pitched, followed by a scream, more barking, and then someone shouting. I had to find out what it was. I ran down the steps, along the waterfront, and jumped over the low wall.

A little stone jetty jutted out into the river and a small dog was tied to one of the posts. A boy stood a short distance from it, a pile of stones beside him. He was amusing himself by aiming them deliberately at the terrified creature. Just as I came up, a girl picked herself up from the gravelly shore and hurled herself at him.

"Stop! You cruel beast!" she was yelling. "Stop it, d'you hear?"

The boy threw her away from him and the dog cried out pitifully as another stone hit it. Its tormentor laughed aloud.

Perhaps because I'd once known it myself in the orphanage, I've always hated to see small, defenseless creatures tortured.

I shouted at the boy to stop his cruel tricks. His only reply was to hurl one of the stones at me. That was enough. I launched myself at him and we went down together, rolling over and over on the muddy strand.

He was small but tough, far stronger and more experienced than I was. He fought savagely. I managed to get in some good punches but he clawed himself around somehow and got me on my back. He had his hands knotted in my hair and the pain was so agonizing that I shut my eyes. I was trying desperately to break his hold when quite suddenly I was free.

Painfully I opened my eyes and saw a look of sheer terror on my enemy's face. Someone had gripped him by the shoulder. He scrambled to his feet and a second later was running faster than seemed possible, with the help of a good kick in the backside. I sat up half dazed, staring at a face I knew, a wild, dark, merry face. I didn't know whether to thank him or whether the moment had come when I must fight out my own personal quarrel with my rescuer.

"Filthy little tyke!" he said. "He never learns!" And he turned to look down at me. The dark face broke into a grin. "You again! By Jiminy, we can't keep away from each other, can we? Better take your dog and get clear. He might come back!"

"Who are you?" I had scrambled to my knees, and the words forced themselves out of me.

The black eyes narrowed, the mouth sneered. "Who knows? Who cares?" he said. Without pausing any longer, he vaulted the stone wall.

"Wait! Come back!" I called after him, but he ran across the steps and went up the alley before I pulled myself to my feet.

The girl had untied the string and was kneeling beside the dog, examining its wounds.

I said crossly, "Why don't you take more care of your pet?"

"It's not mine," she replied indignantly. "I wish it were.

I just couldn't bear to see it hurt." She stood up, still holding the string by which the dog was tied. "I'd like to keep it, but my mother wouldn't be pleased. Here, you'd better take this." She came close to me, putting the cord in my hand and smiling at me sweetly. "You know, you really were very brave."

I'd never had anything to do with girls and didn't like them much. I mumbled something and looked away uncomfortably.

She said in a grown-up kind of voice, "I'm afraid I mustn't stay. I have to go now," and walked away from me toward the theater steps.

I think at any other time I might have stopped her and asked more questions. She wasn't like any girl I'd ever seen before, and after all, it was she who had been brave, not me. Her dress was torn and there was mud on her face where she had been thrown down, but she had made no fuss. But my mind was so full of the boy. I was so occupied with wondering if I could somehow force him into confessing what he had done, that I let her go without another word.

It was the dog that attracted my attention. It was very small and thin, with a rough gray coat and eyes like shining brown pebbles behind a tangled fringe of hair. Blood was trickling from a cut above its ear, but it was tugging impatiently on the string. Out of sheer curiosity and because somehow I felt a link between us, I let myself follow him.

The dog trotted down the strand and turned sharply up one of the alleys. I had never seen this part of the city before. Once, my uncle had told me, this had been a terrible district called Alsatia where thieves and criminals and even murderers were said to live out of reach of the law. Only the foolhardy ever ventured into it alone or unarmed. But the great fire had burned them out and now the district lay empty with broken-down roofs, charred timbers, bare, scarred walls, and great piles of black, stinking garbage.

The little dog went gaily before me up one alley and down another, then abruptly dived down a small flight of steps. He pushed open a door which swung crazily on its hinges. I was just about to follow when I stopped.

On the wooden doorpost was painted a red cross, faded now but still easily seen—the red cross that forbade entrance, that proclaimed this had once been a house cursed with the plague. Horror crept through me, and involuntarily I stepped back. The little dog tugged at the string, looking back at me and whining, and I tried to take firm hold of myself. After all, nearly eight years had gone by, the fire had come and gone. Only cowards are frightened of old things long past. My uncle would have laughed at such foolishness. I took a deep breath, thrust open the door, and went in.

Then I stared about me, unable to believe my eyes. Outside, the roof had fallen in and the walls were black and gutted. But here in some strange way was a basement room quite untouched. The little dog pulled free. It scampered across the room and jumped on the low truckle bed in one corner. Its bright eyes watched me almost as if it were inviting me to stay and share its refuge.

I looked all around, expecting at any moment to see someone come out of the shadows, but then I realized that everything—the table, the stools, the chest—was buried in thick, furry dust. The floor was strewn with dirt and ash. Somehow when the inhabitants fled the fire, the little dog must have been forgotten. Miraculously it had escaped and this room was still its home. Outside, it must have found food and water, but it came back day after day, month after month, year after year, still looking for the loved master who would never come again. Of course I didn't think all this out at once. It came to me slowly in the next few days.

It was very quiet in the room. I missed the noise of Bridewell Court, the sound of voices and the clatter of everyday living. The silence was frightening. It was an eerie place and I shivered. I felt an urge to run away, but the dog leaped down and ran across to me. It jumped up at me, pawing at my coat, pushing its cold nose against my hand. I picked it up, glad to feel the little warm body and the eager tongue that licked my face and hands. It was only then that I realized what had happened. I had found my refuge. Here I could live in safety till I found a way to rescue my Uncle Jeremy.

Chapter 4

I Meet Henry Again

I fetched my bundle from the waterman's hut and, though I told Walt Budge that I had found somewhere to live, I thought it best not to tell him where, in case anyone came asking after me.

I was curiously happy in that lonely basement in Ram Alley with only Rags for company. I'd called the little dog Ragamuffin because of his rough, shaggy coat. Maybe it's foolish to think so, but I am sure he liked it and accepted me as the master he had been waiting for.

When I had wiped off the thick dust and explored every corner, I found all sorts of things in that room, pots to drink out of and pans to cook in. Perhaps they had survived by some freak of the fire, or perhaps someone else had taken refuge there and brought them in. I never knew. I could even bring in wood from outside and light a fire on the hearth to toast a herring or roast a potato. Uncle Jeremy had taught me how to do that. It was something we often did when funds ran short. It was like being on a picnic and I was rather proud of myself for managing so well, although of course there were frightening moments.

The first night, as I lay on the truckle bed with Rags curled up beside me, I woke up suddenly. All round me there were eerie sounds and scurryings. Rats, I thought, but I heard whispers too, soft and sibilant, though I could not make out the words. Ghosts of all those long dead people, perhaps. I shivered and dived under the dusty blankets. Next morning I realized that many homeless creatures lived in the ruins, beggars like myself, who crept out only at night, and I made sure of the bolt on my door.

You see, the whole city was being rebuilt after the fire, and some day of course they would work in here, too, but for the moment it was like an island that had been forgotten, and no one would bother about me or look to find me here. At least that's what I told myself, but I was wrong, quite wrong.

It was about a week later, after what had been a very exciting day, that it happened.

I'd been wonderfully lucky at the theater. The doorkeeper took a fancy to me and I found myself called upon to run a dozen errands. I began to recognize some of the actors who went in and out of the doors—Master Betterton, for instance, very serious and always in a hurry; and Master Sandeman, a lanky beanpole of a man with so quaint and ugly a face that he could never play anything but villains. The doorkeeper told me that the one time he appeared as a heroic character he was hissed off the stage. He gave me as much as a shilling one morning simply for smiling at him.

On this particular day a young lady arrived whom I'd never noticed before, and I thought I'd never seen anyone so pretty. She was carried in a sedan chair, with a gentleman walking beside it. When she stepped out in her rose-colored silk gown with her shining brown-gold hair and friendly smile, she so dazzled me that I had eyes for no one else.

As she moved toward the door, her embroidered gloves fell to the ground and I picked them up and ran after her.

She thanked me as she took them out of my hand. "I am forever doing that," she said, laughing merrily. "London must be strewn with my lost gloves." Then quite suddenly she said, "Boy, have you ever seen a play?"

"Never," I answered.

"Well, then, you shall have that pleasure this very afternoon, shan't he, my lord?" And she glanced up at the gentleman who had come up beside her after paying the chair men.

I followed her look and froze where I stood. It was Lord Maltravers in a fine blue coat laced with silver, swinging his gold-topped cane. His eyes rested on me for a moment and I stood paralyzed, unable to stir. But I needn't have feared. He was far too occupied with the lady to be concerned with an urchin who ran errands at the stage door.

He swung off his feathered hat, almost sweeping the ground with it, so low did he bow. "For you, Melanie, as you know well, I would sell everything I have and beggar myself."

"There's no need for that," she said, rather coldly I thought. "Just give him the price of a ticket." And she swept in the door.

He fumbled in his pocket, threw me a coin, and hurried after her.

That was how I came to be sitting in a fine seat among

the quality, seeing my first play. The inside of the theater was very grand, all painted in red and gold, with a great arch over the stage and two gilt statues holding up the coat of arms of the King's brother, the Duke of York. But when the curtain drew back, I forgot everything but the actors.

It was a tragic story about a Danish Prince whose father had been treacherously murdered by his wicked uncle. My pretty lady was the girl he loved, who went mad when he rejected her. In white satin with her hair flowing free, she scattered flowers and sang sad songs so enchantingly that I could not take my eyes from her.

There were other splendid scenes too, duels that held me spellbound and a ghost in armor, so terrifying in the silvery light that even Prince Hamlet's face shone greenish-white. I felt my skin creep and my breath choke in my throat.

I came out in a daze. I could think of nothing else. I knew at last what I wanted to be . . . not a sailor, not a draper's assistant or a dull apprentice, but an actor! An actor in black velvet like Master Betterton, or in gold and scarlet like the King, an actor who held a whole theater full of people entranced, rocking with laughter or with tears running down their cheeks, an actor who could fight with sword and dagger as magnificently as any soldier and die like one of the heroes in the old ballads. Of course at that time I understood only half the lines, but the beauty of them stirred me and sang through my mind as I went on my homeward way.

If thou didst ever hold me in thy heart,
Absent thee from felicity awhile,

And in this harsh world draw thy breath in pain,
To tell my story.

Harsh world . . . I knew about that, all right. Somehow, when Hamlet had spoken those words, I had thought of my Uncle Jeremy and tears had stung my eyes.

I was humming one of Ophelia's pretty tunes when I reached my alley. I ran down the steps and flung open the door. Then I stood still, the melody dying on my lips.

The room was a wreck. Everything in it had been overturned and torn apart. Furniture, blankets, pots, pans, food —all were heaped in one vast muddle in the center of the floor. It was worse, far worse than when I had first seen it.

The shock was so tremendous that for an instant I couldn't move. Then I remembered Rags. He always ran to greet me, and now he was nowhere to be seen. I called, but there was no answering bark. I ran out into the yard at the back, calling more and more frantically. I think that was the worst of all. To lose him now would be more than I could bear.

I raced back into the house and stopped abruptly. Someone was standing in the middle of the room. It was a moment before I recognized her. It was the girl from the waterside. She was turning slowly, looking from one corner to the other. Then she said calmly, "What a shocking muddle you live in!"

It made me furiously angry. I resented her coming. I shouted at her, "Go away! What's it to do with you? I don't want you here."

She didn't move. "Don't be silly. I'll help you to put it straight."

"I wish you'd go away. I don't want any help."

She turned to look at me. "Are all boys as rude as you? I followed you from the theater because I thought it would be nice to be friends. I'll go if you like, but at least you might tell me what you have done with the little dog."

At that, all my misery came flooding back. "He's gone," I said hopelessly. "Someone has done all this out of spite, and they've taken Rags too."

"Perhaps they haven't," she said. "Perhaps he was just frightened and ran away to hide. Perhaps they've shut him up somewhere. I'll help you look, if you like."

The search took a long while, but she was right. We found him at last, far away up the alley, shut into an outside shed, most likely by the same hand that had torn my room to shreds. He could have starved to death if we had not hunted for him and heard him whining and scratching at the door.

We went back together, and on the steps the girl paused and looked at me. "Would you really rather I went away? I will if you like."

I was silent, half hoping she'd stay and yet not wanting to admit it.

"Well, anyway," she went on, "we might as well know each other's name. Mine's Henry. What's yours?"

"It can't be Henry," I objected, irritated because she seemed to take so much for granted. "It's a boy's name."

"I know." She made a little grimace. "It's short for Henrietta. I like it better." She giggled infectiously, and rather against my will, I found myself grinning too.

"I'm Tom," I said. "Tom Hawke." And we shook hands on it.

It took us a long time to put the room into any sort of order, and I must say the girl worked very hard. I think on my own I might have given up in despair, but she didn't and she suggested we have a race to see who could get the most done first. It did make everything more fun.

We were halfway through when she pounced on the lute, which miraculously had escaped damage.

"Can you play it, Tom?"

"Not really . . ."

"I can. Listen." And she began to march up and down, strumming out a popular air.

It was the old ballad of "Barbara Allen," one of my uncle's favorites. I told you I had a quick ear. In a few moments I forgot my shyness and was fitting the words to it. I sang it right to the end. But then I saw Henry standing still, staring at me in astonishment, and I blushed to the roots of my hair.

"Why, you can sing, Tom," she exclaimed.

"No, I can't . . . at least . . ."

"It was lovely," she persisted. "Much better than the singing boys at the theater."

"Don't be silly," I protested, but I did feel pleased in spite of myself. It was fun having someone to share things with. We laughed a lot, until I made the discovery. You see, I had buried the black box in a chest under a pile of old clothes. They had all been turned out and torn to ribbons and the box was gone.

I tried to hide my dismay, but Henry must have seen the look on my face. "What's the matter?" she asked.

"The money," I said stupidly. "It's gone."

"Perhaps it's just dropped down somewhere."

"No, it was in a box."

"Was it very much?"

"All we had in the world."

"I'm sorry, really sorry," she said with quick sympathy. "I know how awful it is to be without any money. It happens to my mother and me sometimes."

We were sitting on the floor side by side and for the first time I looked at her, really looked, I mean. She had very dark blue eyes and light brown hair that fell glossy and straight to her waist. She was not like any of the girls I had seen in Bridewell Court. Her dress was of flowered silk with lace and ribbons, very pretty and rich, even though there were dirty smudges on the skirt and on her face too. I wondered if she could possibly know what it felt like to have no more than a few coppers in your pocket.

She interrupted my thoughts by saying softly, "Tom, are you all alone? I mean, isn't there anyone else?"

I shook my head. "No. My father and mother died when I was very little." I was just about to tell her about Uncle Jeremy when she went on without waiting for me. "I believe I know who might have done this to you."

"Who?"

"That boy . . . on the waterside . . . do you remember? The one that was tormenting Rags."

"But how could he know?"

She turned to look at me. "Didn't you realize? He used to run errands at the theater till the day the doorkeeper found him stealing from the actors' dressing room and gave him a whipping. He's been hanging around ever since. He must have seen you and been jealous. He could have followed you home."

I really had been very stupid. I should have guessed.

Henry had scrambled to her feet. She was clapping her hands in excitement. "I've got a simply splendid idea. Why don't you come to the King's Theatre in Drury Lane?

There's lots and lots of work to be found there. Very rich people go in and out all the time, the King himself sometimes. You could work as a linkboy."

"A linkboy?"

"You know," she said impatiently. "They wait outside with their torches and light people home after the play. There's never enough. You might even be taken on at the theater. They're always wanting extra help backstage. And the doorkeeper there is a friend of mine."

"How do you know so much?" I asked rather crossly, because she was taking altogether too much on herself. She seemed to think I must fall in with anything she suggested.

"Because my mother's an actress of course, silly. She was in the play at the Dorset Garden this afternoon, but only because Mistress Betterton, who plays Ophelia, was suddenly taken sick. She really belongs to the King's Company."

"Your mother? My pretty lady?" I was staring at her in surprise. Such an idea had never once crossed my mind. She seemed much too young to have a daughter nearly as old as myself.

"Oh, do you think she's pretty?" repeated Henry carelessly. "I suppose she is, really. My Lord Maltravers thinks so."

"I suppose you know him too?" I said, rather sarcastically.

"Of course I do. He is always on our doorstep swearing he's in love with her."

"In love?" I still couldn't quite take everything in. "But what about your father?"

"He's dead," said Henry flatly.

"Oh, I'm sorry . . ." I began, but she cut me short.

"It's all right. It was a long time ago. I hardly remember him."

"Is your mother going to marry Lord Maltravers?"

"Marry him! Don't be stupid. An actress marry a great man like that! I don't think she likes him much. I know I don't." And she wrinkled her nose in disgust. "Tom, do come to Drury Lane. We might be able to see each other sometimes."

I hesitated. So much had happened, and I was still dazed at losing the money and at finding out that her mother was who she was and was somehow linked with the man I thought of as our enemy. I was glad I had said nothing about Uncle Jeremy. Perhaps if I were to do as she suggested, if I were to get to know them better, I could find out more.

"All right," I said at last. "I'll come. I've got to make a living somehow."

"Goody," she said, and gave me a dazzling smile. "I get awfully lonely sometimes when Mother is so much at the theater." She was at the door before I could scramble to my feet. "I must go now. Goodbye, Tom. Don't forget, will you?"

I ran after her because I thought I ought to have offered to walk home with her, but by the time I reached the top of the steps, she had vanished down one of the alleys. She was always independent, as I was to find out.

Chapter 5

My Uncle Is Tried

The public benches in the criminal court hard by Newgate were crammed full on the day of my uncle's trial. I'd pushed my way in and was wedged beside an enormously fat woman with a basket on her lap. The sharp corners kept digging into me. On the other side sat a little thin man whose bony elbow was rammed into my ribs, but I scarcely noticed it, so anxious was I about my uncle.

I thought the first case would never come to an end. A grocer had been accused of giving short weight and cheating his customers. I certainly felt glad that I was not apprenticed to such a mean, nasty, rat-faced creature. He was sentenced to a whipping and then to stand in the pillory. I'd seen men in that before. It was a post topped by a board that would clamp around his neck and wrists, holding him firm. Then all his furious customers could pelt him with bad eggs, rotten fruit, or any other garbage they could lay their hands on. Serve him right, I thought, but my eyes were not really on him. They were on the judges.

There were three of them, but the chief one, who sat in the center, had a red, brutal face and a big fleshy nose under his white wig. This must be "Old Beaky," the hanging judge the boy had spoken of. On the desk in front of him lay a small nosegay of herbs and sweet-scented flowers, as was customary to protect him from the heat and stench of the crowded courtroom.

The people around me were hooting and jeering as the grocer was led out. The flowers leaped into the air as the judge brought his fist down on the desk, yelling for order.

When all was quiet again, it was the turn of my uncle. My heart missed a beat when the two warders brought him in, shuffling a little because of the heavy chain that clasped his ankles.

He stood upright in the dock, his head held high, his dark brown hair tied back in the simple fashion he always used. Somehow he contrived to look neat and clean as usual and, in his plain brown coat, he had a proud, free air. A murmur of sympathy ran through the court, and the fat woman beside me bent forward to peer at him.

"It's a cruel shame," she muttered, "that such as he with the look of an angel should go thieving and robbing honest folk."

It was on the tip of my tongue to fly out at her for a wicked liar, but perhaps it was a good thing that I didn't draw attention to myself. The next moment the first witness had gone into the box.

I had been brought up to speak the truth and I had never in my life listened to such a tangled mass of lies as came from the men and women who now stepped forward.

They swore on oath that they had seen my uncle sidle up to Lord Maltravers, described how he had taken the purse, how they had watched the gold being passed to an accomplice—all kinds of false tales. I was bewildered. Did they imagine it? Did they hear it said so many times that they really believed they had seen it? Or were they merely inspired by jealousy and spite? I never knew.

When the judge began to put his questions, my uncle spoke out bold and clear, telling exactly what had happened, but there was no one to support his story, no one to speak of his honesty. What had happened to the letter I had taken to Master Pepys? Had the clerk forgotten it? I felt sick, because somehow it seemed as if I had failed him.

It was only a week since the black box had been stolen from me, and without a bribe the turnkey at Newgate had refused to let me in to see my uncle, though I pleaded until I was hoarse. I watched my uncle, eagerly trying to catch his eye, and presently I noticed that he gave a quick look around the court as if searching for someone. Then he smiled and I knew that he had seen me, though he made no other sign of recognition.

Now a new witness had stepped into the box, a gentleman in a fine black coat, disdainfully holding a lace handkerchief to his nose as if he despised the vulgar company in which he found himself. After he had been sworn in, the prosecutor said respectfully, "You are Master Nathaniel Leigh, servant to my Lord Maltravers?"

"I am his secretary," replied the gentleman haughtily. "And sent by my master to bear witness against the prisoner there in the dock. Ten years ago Jeremy Hawke was in service with my lord and a large sum of money disappeared. Grave suspicion rested on this man, but before the matter could be fully investigated, he fled from the house, grievously wounding the porter on the gate, and was not seen again until my lord recognized him on Cheapside, still at his old thieving tricks."

"He lies!" My uncle's voice rang sharply through the court. "He lies, and his master too. I never stole any money, and that they know full well. It was a false accusation leveled at me because I had unfortunately incurred his displeasure about quite another matter."

"Do you dare to question my lord's honor?" shouted the man in the box angrily.

"And why shouldn't I?" replied my uncle. "Is he God that every word he utters must be the truth?"

At this, an uproar broke out in the court. Everyone seemed to be taking sides. People shouted, argued, and yelled at one another. In vain the clerk banged with his staff on the floor.

"Silence!" roared the judge at last, his red face turning a dull purple. "Silence! If you cannot keep quiet, I will have the court cleared."

When the noise died down, he frowned under his heavy brows, looking from Master Leigh to my uncle. He said irritably, "What is this matter that you speak of between you and my Lord Maltravers?"

My uncle hesitated, then he answered firmly. "It is personal and it has nothing to do with the present charge against me."

"Obstinacy brings its own reward," remarked the judge unpleasantly, and turned to the man in the black coat, who leaned back with a nasty smile on his face.

"Can you bring proof that this is the same man who robbed your master in days gone by?"

SOIT QVI MAL Y PENSE

"Certainly I can, m'lud," he replied eagerly. "There are others in my lord's service, ready and waiting to swear to his identity on oath."

"Very well. Produce them without delay. And another thing," the judge went on, turning to the constable who had arrested my uncle. "There is constant talk of a boy in this case, an accomplice it would appear of this rascal in the dock. Where, pray, is he, or did you let him slip through your fingers, eh? Answer me that."

As the constable stammered out a reply, I shrank back against my fat companion, trying to look as inconspicuous as possible. All of a sudden a woman's voice, shrill and denouncing, interrupted from the public benches below me.

"There," she screamed, "there he is, sir, the very boy. See him, bold as brass, the young varmint, and ran off from me just like his uncle. Me, who've been like a mother to them both these two years. A pair of false rogues, both of 'em."

It was Mistress Larkin, standing up among the spectators and pointing at me, her little black eyes full of spite and malice.

The constable started toward me, but I didn't wait. The thin man at my side made a grab at my arm, but I vaulted over the bench and tried to thrust my way through the mob behind. At first they were like a solid block between me and safety, then quite suddenly their mood changed and they were on my side. They parted in front of me. Someone said, "Run, boy. Go on, run!" And as I went through, they closed in behind me and I was passed from one to the other till I reached the door and tore down the staircase.

There was a shout behind me and the man at the entrance put out an arm to stop me. I kicked out at him and must have caught him on the shin. He gave a groan of pain and let go and I was out in the street. I darted across the road, narrowly avoiding a coach and horses, which luckily blocked my pursuers, who raged on the other side. I sped through the arch of Newgate and down Holborn, running as fast as I could till I reached the maze of twisting alleys leading down to the Church of St. Giles. There, I thought, I would be safe.

Seven Dials was a squalid district of broken-down wooden tenements. I had never walked there alone before, and I was a little scared by the hard, suspicious stares of the ragged men and women as I hurried through the lanes, but what had happened at the trial had driven everything else out of my mind.

What could my uncle have done to earn the hatred of Lord Maltravers? I knew he wasn't guilty, but what could we do against so powerful an enemy? For the first time I felt utterly helpless. I could have sat down and wept, but that would only have been childish. I tried hard to pull myself together and went hurrying on my way to Drury Lane.

Whether it was because of Henry, I don't know—I'd not seen her since the evening at Ram Alley—but the door-keeper at the Theatre Royal had been grudgingly friendly. There were always other boys hanging around looking for a chance to earn a good tip, but he picked on me more often than most. I knew I was getting black looks, but I didn't care. I had learned one lesson in these last few days. If you didn't push yourself, you got nowhere.

"Wherever have you got to, boy?" grumbled the door-keeper when I came panting up. "It's three of the clock already and those devils of boys all run off somewhere.

Here's been Mistress Gilbert plaguing the life out of me to carry a message for her, and me rushed off my feet and not knowing where to turn. Go in now, quickly. I can't leave here. It's the door at the end of the passage. Go quietly . . . And don't forget to knock," he called after me.

There was a shriek and a stifled giggle when I tapped. Then someone said, "Come on in." The door was opened and I was pulled inside. I found myself facing a young woman with a mop of dark curls and merry sparkling eyes, clad only in her petticoat and low-necked bodice.

I had never seen so many half-clothed females in all my life and I didn't know where to look. I wanted to run out, but the curly-haired girl was between me and the door, her bright eyes mocking me.

"Well," she said, "speak up, or have you swallowed your tongue?"

"The doorkeeper said you wanted a letter taken," I faltered.

"Oh, he did, did he? Well, well, girls, did you hear that? That's as good an excuse as any to break into the ladies' dressing room. So young and so saucy. Well, malapert, shall I give you a kiss for it? Shall I?" And she advanced so purposefully that I took a step backward, tripped over a stool, and went sprawling on the floor.

I picked myself up to gales of laughter. The room seemed to be crammed with costumes hanging around the walls, baskets spilling over, stockings, shoes, wigs, make-up, pots of ale, all in a glorious muddle, and to cap it all, half a dozen giggling young women standing all around me. I wished I were anywhere else.

"Shame on you, Nell, tormenting the poor boy," said a cool voice and my pretty lady came out of a corner.

"Don't take any notice of her. She's nothing but a tease. I'm the one who wants a letter delivered. Will you do it for me?"

"Yes . . . yes, of course, ma'am."

"Can you read?"

I nodded and she put a folded paper in my hands with a silver shilling. "The direction is written on it."

I couldn't take my eyes from her. She looked so lovely in her satin gown with flowers and feathers in her soft brown hair.

"Mistress Gilbert . . . your call," shouted a voice outside, and someone banged on the door.

She gave a little shriek. "Oh heavens, I shall miss my entrance." And she fled from the room.

"Look at him," scoffed the one they called Nell. "Standing there for all the world like a stuffed image. He's lost his heart for sure and to our pretty Melanie. She's not for you, my little one." She came close, trying to peer at the letter in my hand. "Who has she written to, eh? Come on, show . . . we're all friends here."

"No," I said, "no, I won't. It's private."

"Oh, hoity-toity! All up in the air, are we? Go on then, be off with you, boy, this is no place for you." And I was bundled unceremoniously into the passage.

Out in the street, I stared down at the folded paper in my hand. It was addressed to the noble Edward Denham, Earl Maltravers, at his house opposite St. Paul's Church in Covent Garden.

That hateful name seemed to haunt me. What had she written to him? It's silly, but I think I was even a little jealous. You see, I had only a hazy memory of my own mother, and Mistress Melanie was exactly as I had imagined her so often in my dreams.

I must admit that I approached the fine house in the piazza with some hesitation, but there was nought to fear. A footman in a handsome livery snatched the letter out of my hand and slammed the door shut in my face.

But the strange happenings of that eventful day were not yet over. After the play was done, it was already growing dusk. The doorkeeper allowed me to light my torch of tow soaked in pitch with his tinder box, and I found myself walking in front of an elderly couple across the fields to their house in St. Martin's Lane. I rather enjoyed it, though the fresh wind drove the stinking black smoke of the torch back into my face.

With part of Mistress Melanie's shilling I bought myself a big meat pie and set off homeward, eating as I went. It was now quite dark, and when I crossed the piece of waste ground where Drury Lane comes into the Strand, I heard footsteps padding behind me. In sudden panic I started to run. The footsteps came faster. I heard others joining in. I doubled my speed, but suddenly something was thrown over my head. I struggled in the thick stifling folds, but strong arms pulled the sacking tight, clamping my hands to my sides, and despite all my efforts, I was marched away over the rough ground with no notion at all of where I was going.

Chapter 6

I Meet the Link Boys

All sorts of horrible thoughts went racing through my mind. There were boys who were press-ganged into the Navy, boys who were kidnapped and shipped off to outlandish places like Morocco or Algiers to be sold as slaves, boys who just disappeared and whose bodies were mysteriously washed up in the Thames. I think I died a thousand deaths and all of them frightful. Then I was stumbling down a flight of wooden steps. The air became warm and stuffy after the freshness of the night, and a voice said sharply, "Tie his arms and legs."

Stout rope was lashed around my ankles, and my wrists were tied firmly behind my back. Then the sack was whisked off my head. It was very dark and a moment or two went by before I could see anything. I seemed to be in a cellar. The one window had been boarded up and the room was lit only by a lantern and three tallow dips stuck in their own grease.

I looked around me, and instead of the villainous faces I had expected, I saw five boys ranged in a semicircle opposite me, four of them no older than myself. In the center, sitting on an upturned barrel casually swinging his long legs, was that same maddening youth I was beginning to know so well.

The very fact that I had been so frightened and now felt a sudden flood of relief made me furiously angry. I made a rush at him, stupidly forgetting that my ankles were tied, so that I stumbled, fell flat on my face, and couldn't get up again.

There was a burst of laughter from the boys. Trembling and humiliated, I shouted at them, "Why have you brought me here? What have I ever done to you?"

"Shall we tell him? Shall we teach him a lesson, Josh? Shall we?" asked one of the boys. Small, thin, and wiry, he had a pinched white face and hair the color of newly washed carrots.

"Shut up, Rick."

Joshua, for that is what I must call him now, slid off the barrel and took a step toward me, spreading his legs, his hands on his hips. "What's your name, youngster?"

"What's that to you?"

"We'll get along a lot better if you'll only stop shouting," said the boy reasonably. "Here, some of you, give me a hand to set him on his feet. I know your uncle's name, but I'm cursed if I'm going to call you Master Hawke. We have no handles to our names here, do we, boys?"

There was a roar of agreement and two of the boys hauled me roughly to my feet and stood me upright. I looked around the circle of intent faces watching me, their eyes glittering.

"I'm Tom," I said at last, trying to sound proud and defiant. "What do you want with me?"

"What do you want with me?" mimicked another boy jeeringly. He was short and round as a tub of lard, a mass of fair, lank hair hanging around a face red as a Dutch cheese, and I knew I'd seen him outside the theater. "Why did you come butting in, snatching the bread out of our mouths? This is our pitch, has been all this past year."

"Hold your tongue!" interrupted Joshua sternly. "Who asks the questions? Who is the leader, you or me?"

"Sorry, Josh," mumbled the boy humbly. "I wasn't thinking."

"Right, Gil. Well, don't forget it again. Now you"—he moved a step toward me—"come on now, out with it. Why did you leave your own pitch down by Dorset Garden and come bursting into ours, eh? Didn't your uncle ever teach you not to grab at what ain't yours?"

"I have to live, haven't I? Same as you. The streets are free. You don't own them." And I looked from one to the other, not wanting to confess about the robbery or that it was Henry who had given me the idea.

I raised my head, facing up to the leader himself. "And who are you to preach about grabbing what's not yours? If it hadn't been for you, none of this would have happened to me."

Joshua did not answer. He simply snapped his fingers and one of the boys disappeared into the shadows. In a moment he was back with something under his arm. He set it down between us.

I stared at it incredulously. It was the black box.

"Have you seen that before?" asked Joshua.

"But how did you get it?" Then I glared at him accusingly. "Was it you who stole it, after all, and not him?"

"You're too innocent to live," remarked Joshua scornfully. He kicked open the lid with his foot. "Can't swear that all the money's there, but there's some of it, at any rate. Did you think young Con wouldn't watch your every movement? He used to be one of us till we threw him out and wanted none of him. I've kept an eye on him ever since."

"You mean you knew about me . . . and about Ram Alley?"

"Why not? We have our spies. It was easy."

It was all so strange. I was still bewildered, not sure what he meant or what they intended to do with me, but at the same time very curious.

"Why?" I asked. "Why did you throw him out?"

He looked me up and down before he answered. "He broke one of our rules, that's why. He stole from Rick here, picked his pocket one night after he'd had a good haul. As neat a job as ever I saw, but it's not allowed. The world's full of the rich and it's full of fools and if you can get some of the gold off one or other of them, good luck to you, but not from your pals and not from those who're as out of fortune's favor as you are. That's a rat's trick. It would be the noose round his neck and the high jump for such as he if I had my way, but I'm not old Beaky, so out he went and all hands against him."

He spoke quietly, but it struck a chill through me. There was silence for a few moments. The four boys did not move. They watched steadily, waiting for their leader's verdict. He was looking at me thoughtfully.

"Now, comrades," he said at length. "He's no more sense than a babe in arms. He'll not last a week on his own. So what shall we do with him? Shall we leave him to fight his own battles, or shall we make him one of us?"

The boys looked at one another. Then Rick spoke. "What did he mean, Josh, when he said you were to blame?"

"It so happens that his uncle's in Newgate," he said reluctantly. "How the devil was I to know he'd . . ." He broke off and then went on harshly. "At any rate, it's up to you all to say . . . you first, Rick."

"I think he should take Con's place."

"Gil?"

"Aye, mebbe he'll do. If you're sure he'll not go blabbing."

"Tim?"

"I don't like it. He's different from us. He speaks different, he looks different."

Tim was so thin he looked like two planks tied together. He wore ragged breeches and tattered shirt and no shoes or stockings on his bare, dirty feet.

"Phil?" went on Joshua, turning to the last of the boys. His shoulders were hunched and he had a hump on his back. He moved forward with a limping step and his hand held a crutch under his left arm.

"I say no." And he looked at me with hostility. "I agree with Tim. We don't want none of his sort."

Joshua ran his eye around the circle of faces.

"That's two for and two against, so it's up to me to give the casting vote. I say yes if . . .—and he paused dramatically—"if he passes the test."

"Aye, the test!" All four voices sounded gleeful. "Let him pass the test, then we shall see."

"Right. Prepare it, then."

I was pushed to one side while they scattered to all corners of the basement. Very soon they were back, carrying old boxes and broken-down chairs and tables. In no time they had built two crazy structures a good eight or nine feet high. Then two of them brought a long plank not more than ten inches wide and balanced it precariously between the makeshift posts.

"Untie his legs, hoist him up, and blindfold him," commanded Joshua, and I realized with a sick feeling inside me what they wanted me to do.

I had always hated heights. My head went dizzy if I dared to look down from our attic window, and now I would have to walk across this unsteady, trembling, swaying bridge with my hands tied behind me and my eyes blinded. I felt sweat prickle on my forehead and break out on my palms. I couldn't do it, I couldn't. Something inside me was screaming silently, "No, no, no!"

Then I saw Joshua watching me, a mocking smile on the thin lips. I saw each of the four boys waiting for me to hesitate and to call me coward. Better to try and fall. Better to break my neck than be laughed at as a weakling.

"Ready?" asked Joshua crisply.

I nodded, not trusting myself to keep my voice steady. They unlashed my ankles. Then two of them helped me to climb up onto that rocky perch. I was thankful to see that Gil and Rick were on each side, holding the plank steady. Then they set me on the edge of it and tied a scarf around my eyes.

"One . . . two . . . three . . ." counted Joshua slowly. "Now! Forward!"

Quite honestly, I think it was the worst moment of my whole life. One false step and I would plunge into space and crash to the floor. There was absolute silence. I swear I could hear my heart beating. Then I took one step forward.

With my hands tied I had nothing with which to balance myself, yet somehow I had to remain firm and steady. I took another step, and then another. There was a moment when I stopped, shaking, quite unable to move either forward or back. Joshua told me afterward that they were sure I would topple over and he and Tim stood below ready to break my fall. But, by some miracle, courage came back and I did the last few paces at a rush.

Then everything changed. Willing hands helped me to the floor. Tim undid the blindfold, Rick untied my hands. They crowded around, laughing, patting me on the back. I, who had never known what it was like to have friends of my own age, was suddenly one of a family. It was exciting and I felt a great wave of pure happiness. Like one of the knights in the old tales, I had won my spurs and now felt the equal of anyone.

We had a merry supper. It was only bread and hard cheese, with a can of thin ale passed from one to the other, a few sips for each and the greater part for Joshua, but to me the company made it as good as a feast.

The boys didn't talk much about themselves, but like me they had no parents, no relatives to care for them. I guess they felt for Joshua just as I felt for Uncle Jeremy.

By the time we had finished, it was quite dark outside and my new friends insisted on accompanying me to Ram Alley. Rags set up such a barking that I thought he would rouse the whole district, but he calmed down as soon as Phil knelt beside him. For some reason, the lame boy was the only one who still looked at me with hostility. I would have snatched the little dog away from him, but then could not. Phil was hugging him, his face joyful as Rags gaily licked it.

The others explored the room, examining everything, while Joshua stood in the middle surveying them, his hands on his hips.

"Well, youngster, you're snug as a bug, ain't you? You're luckier than some." Then abruptly he moved to the door, commanding his little band. "Come on, boys, enough's enough."

They went racing past him, laughing. "See you tomorrow, Tom," they called back to me, and I waved good night, looking after them happily, Rags tucked under my arm.

Joshua was still standing in the doorway, watching me. "Pleased with ourselves, ain't we?" he said, and the thin lips sneered. "Master Tom's on top of the world and Uncle Jeremy can kick his legs from the gibbet at Tyburn, for all he cares."

I stared at him, my happiness all draining away because he was right. For a little while in the pleasure of the evening, I had forgotten.

"Were you there, in the court?" I breathed.

"Oh yes, I was there while you ran out, bolted like a scared rabbit when that old beldam screeched at you."

He stood there grinning and jeering, when it was he who should have been in the prison. I couldn't bear it any longer. Furiously I made a rush at him, lashing and kicking out, but I didn't stand a chance. In a minute he had overpowered me, twisting my arms behind my back in a vice-like grip that I couldn't break, however hard I struggled.

He held me in front of him, whispering in my ear. "Well, what are you going to do about it, Master Tom, eh?"

"Let me be," I flung back at him. "Why are you tormenting me like this?"

"He could escape," he went on. "Prisoners have escaped even from the condemned cell before now."

He released me and I faced him, the very possibility of escape so taking my breath away that I forgot my anger. "Escape! But how? Could it be done?"

"Oh yes," he said coolly, "I could do it." He leaned back against the doorpost. "But why should I? You don't trust me, do you? I'm only a common cutpurse, a rogue who cares not a pin for anyone but himself."

I think in that moment I began to understand him a little. In his heart he was sorry for what he had done, but he would never admit to it. That would be weakness, and he had to be strong in all things. But all the same, the idea was so dazzling I could not let it slip. "Would you help, Joshua? Would you? You and the boys?"

"The boys will do what I say," he answered with quick pride. "And you too, understand?"

"Yes. I'll do anything, anything . . . if only you can think of a way."

"That's easy," he said, and his gay confidence was infectious. "There are a dozen different ways, and we have time. There's a week or two yet."

Now he was different again, friendly and smiling, his hand on my shoulder. "We'll do it, young Tom. Never fear."

"When?" I asked eagerly. "When, Josh?" I was ready to get started that very night if needs be.

"All in good time. There are one or two things to be thought on first. So long, Tom. See you." He gave my shoulder a hard squeeze and was gone before I could ask even one of the hundreds of questions crowding to my lips.

I was doubtful, distrustful still, when I climbed into my truckle bed, but I felt a faint glimmer of hope. Rags scrambled up beside me and I hugged him.

"We're not alone any more, old fellow. We have friends."

It was a comforting feeling.

Chapter 7

I Sing for My Supper

"I don't believe you've heard a single word I've been saying," grumbled Henry. "Whatever is the matter, Tom?"

"Nothing," I said.

But there was something very much the matter. Two days had gone by, Joshua had vanished without a word, and I didn't dare to say too much about my uncle's escape to the boys, not yet, not without his permission.

"Yes, there is," went on Henry doggedly. "You're sitting there sulky as a bear with a sore back. Don't you want to come to the party tonight?"

"What party?"

"Oh goodness, I knew you weren't listening. Mistress Nell Gwynne is having a party for her birthday," she repeated patiently. "All sorts of people are going to be there."

"What people?"

"Never you mind." She looked mysterious. "There'll be some of the actors from the theater, and my mother, of course. I know Peg, the kitchen maid at Mistress Nell's lodgings," she explained, her eyes sparkling. "She'll let us in and we'll have some of the fine food and enjoy some of the fun."

"But if they see us, won't they be angry?"

"They won't see us, and anyway what does it matter if they do? Don't be such a wet blanket, Tom. Don't you want to be grown-up and do exciting things?"

"Yes, of course I do." I was indignant because it didn't seem right to me that a girl should be more adventurous than I was. "Anyway, shouldn't you be at school this afternoon?" I added nastily.

I knew Henry was supposed to go each day to Master Watchet's Academy for Young Ladies, but whenever she could avoid it without her mother knowing, she did.

"I've told you," she said grandly. "I'm going to be an actress and I can read and speak lines better than any of them. Why should I have to learn to do a lot of silly sums and spend all day with my needle, stitching at my embroidery? Besides, the girls are so stupid. All they think about is keeping their gowns clean, curling their hair, and chattering about the boys they are going to marry."

Henry got up and peered out of the doorway where we had taken shelter from a drenching shower of rain.

"I think it's stopped now. I'm going home," she said in her abrupt way. "I'll meet you outside the theater after the play."

She was already picking her way carefully down the street, holding her skirts high to avoid the river of mud gushing down the gutter.

"Can I bring Rags?" I called after her. "He's miserable if I shut him up all day."

"If you like, but you'll have to hold him tight. Mistress Nell has a spaniel called Tuttie and she's very jealous."

Having something to look forward to certainly helped the time to pass. I don't know how Henry managed to escape her mother, but she was there as she had promised soon after the play ended, and hand in hand we raced up Bow Street and around through the back yard into the kitchen of Mistress Gwynne's lodging.

There was a tremendous bustle going on and it was terribly hot with the most lovely smell of roasting chickens and sizzling pork. Peg was as round and plump as one of her own puddings. She pushed us into a corner while the dishes went in and out, but she made sure we had a taste of everything. Henry and I and Rags stuffed ourselves to bursting with meat and pastry and creamy tarts. I'd not eaten so much since Uncle Jeremy had been arrested. It was wonderful.

But it wasn't only the delicious food. There was a peculiar air of excitement in the kitchen. Peg and the other maids spoke in whispers and kept exchanging glances, and just outside in the passage a fair man in a plain dark coat leaned against the wall with his arms folded and stared very hard at everyone who went in and out.

When the last dish had been carried out and a great bowl of fruit and nuts was being prepared, Peg said quietly, "Now you two, just one peep around the door but that's all, and keep quiet as mice, unless you want me to lose my place."

"Come on," said Henry and grabbed at my hand.

We stole along the passage. The door to the big room

was wide open and a painted screen had been placed partly across it. Hidden behind it, we could see quite easily.

There was a long table at one end, and the guests had drawn back their stools. Mistress Nell, with a man's feathered hat perched on her curls, a rapier under her arm, and her skirts tucked up, was striding up and down, acting the gallant and singing one of the popular ballads in a very comical fashion. I had seen her perform more than once at the theater, so my eye was caught by the company around the table.

There was Charles Hart, who was the leading actor at the Theatre Royal. I thought him even more splendid than Master Betterton. I'd crept into the gallery once and seen him play Alexander. He was so handsome and had such a magnificent air, no king could have acted it better. Then I saw Henry's mother with Lord Maltravers close beside her. As I watched, he put a hand on hers and she snatched it away and turned her back on him. She looked so pale and unhappy, I longed to tell her that, except for my uncle, there was no one I admired so much.

Then my eye fell on the man who sat in the center of the table and I gasped. He wore a plain black coat and silver embroidered waistcoat. He was leaning back in his high-backed, carved chair, long white fingers fiddling with his wine glass. There was no mistaking the dark harsh features, the thin black mustache, the sleepy, half-closed eyes.

Henry nudged me. "Do you see?"

"It can't be," I whispered.

"Yes, it is." She sounded triumphant.

I had never seen him before, but I knew who it was. King Charles himself, here in this ordinary room, only a few feet away from me just like any ordinary person.

I couldn't take my eyes from him. Excitement went

surging through me, and then of course it happened. We had forgotten all about Rags. He had come trotting out of the kitchen after us and, always curious, had poked his nose around the screen to see what was going on. I made a grab at him, but it was too late. An elegant little spaniel came skidding across the polished floor, barking shrilly, and Rags advanced to meet her, tail wagging gaily. But Tuttie took an instant dislike and in a second they were fighting.

Mistress Nell stopped singing and shrieked that her pet would be killed. The guests roared with laughter. Nobody lifted a finger to separate them, and Rags in fine fettle proceeded to teach Tuttie that this was no way to treat a guest.

That was not the worst. The two dogs hit the screen with a bump, it slid to one side and revealed Henry and me, still kneeling on the floor. Mistress Nell uttered a scream of rage and pounced on me, grabbing me by the hair and dragging me into the center of the room.

"You saucy wretch! You poking, prying little beast!" she exclaimed, and gave me a stinging box on the ear.

"Don't do that!" Henry had scrambled to her feet and run after us, pulling at Mistress Nell's uplifted hand. "Don't hit him. It was my fault. I brought him."

"Oh, you did, did you, Miss Impudence? Some trick of your mother's, I'll be bound."

"Henrietta!" Mistress Gilbert had risen to her feet. "Why aren't you at home? Whatever are you thinking of, to come here like this?"

I had managed somehow to free myself and was desperately trying to separate the snarling dogs. I got Rags away and the man from the passage had come in and seized Tuttie, at the same time putting a heavy hand on my shoulder. Henry's mother and Mistress Nell were arguing violently, the guests were laughing, the dogs growling and whining, when a deep voice cut right across the pandemonium.

"Oddsfish, Nell," said the King. "Can't you keep that little brute of yours quiet? She's bitten me once already. I don't want poor Chiffinch damaged for life. It's all right, my dear fellow, let the boy go. I don't think he's going to assassinate me." There was laughter in the pleasant tone. "Is this some new game for our entertainment?"

"Yes," said Henry so boldly that everyone, including His Majesty, turned to look at her. She dropped a little curtsy. "It was my idea. You see, Tom sings so beautifully." She looked around the company with wide, innocent eyes that I was beginning to know always meant mischief. "I thought, you see, that in return for our lovely supper, you would like to hear him."

I was appalled. I couldn't believe my ears. I opened my mouth to protest, and Henry trod heavily on my foot. My exclamation of pain was drowned by Nell's outraged interruption. "Of all the impudent, saucy brats! How dare you force your way in here with your friend from the gutter?"

"He's not," answered Henry furiously. "He's a nice boy, he's . . ." But the King silenced her with a wave of his hand.

"Hush, child. I've a mind to hear this paragon of yours. Such determination and such a pretty face deserve encouragement. Don't you agree, my friends?" His smiling glance took in all the company. "Come then, Master Tom, we are ready and waiting."

I was paralyzed. I couldn't move. There, in front of me, charming and gracious, was the King. I felt everyone's eyes fixed on me and my throat dried up. I tried to say something and only a croak came out.

"Sing 'Barbara Allen,' " hissed Henry in a whisper.

But I couldn't remember a line of it, and as for the melody, it had quite gone out of my head.

Goodness knows what would have happened if Mistress Gilbert hadn't come forward. She was dressed in sea-green silk that evening, and her gold hair hung in curls on her shoulders. She put a gentle hand on my shoulder. "Don't be afraid, Tom. I'll play the spinet for you. Henry, take the little dog from him."

She moved over to the instrument against the wall. I had never seen one like it before. It was a small beautiful box on slim legs with ivory keys, and when her white fingers touched them, a rush of sweet, delicious music ran through the room.

"Come now . . .

> *"In Scarlet town where I was bound*
> *There was a fair maid dwelling . . .*

"Isn't that it?"

She smiled at me invitingly and my courage came back, but she still had to play the opening bars twice through before I could swallow the hard lump in my throat. When I did, I kept my eyes fixed on her. I didn't sing for the King or for any of the grand guests but for her alone, so that the applause at the end startled and confused me.

"Charming, charming." The King was leading the clapping. "A new recruit for you, Master Hart, when the boys' voices break and they croak like bullfrogs in spring."

Charles Hart murmured something and I felt his eyes looking me up and down. The color rushed into my face.

This was such an extraordinary evening, it seemed that anything could happen. Perhaps my dream would come true. Perhaps my singing, which I'd never thought of any value, would carry me on to the stage. For a second my hopes rose high, nearly stifling me. Then common sense came racing back. No doubt they were only teasing, like all great folk, making fun of the poor linkboy who held their horses for a penny and carried the torch before them through the muddy streets, the stinking smoke blowing back and turning him into a blackamoor.

Henry whispered, "Come on, Tom. It's all over. We must go."

But I hesitated. I saw Lord Maltravers stare at me, then lean toward the King. He whispered something and Charles nodded and those dark, sleepy eyes were turned on me.

I don't know what possessed me. It was madness but it seemed a chance that might never come again. There before me was the King of England; in his hands lay the power. One word from him and my uncle would be pardoned, a free man once again. Charles was said to be kind and just. Surely he would believe my story.

I ran forward. I fell on my knees. I poured out the whole tale, the arrest, my uncle's condemnation, all in one jumbled, incoherent muddle. Breathlessly I stammered to an end, but when I raised my eyes, I realized my mistake. The King was frowning. His face was no longer friendly. It had gone stern and cold.

He said, "What is all this to me? I am not the law, and justice must take its course."

All around me, eyes glared with contempt and dislike. I scrambled to my feet and ran out of the room. Henry came after me. She caught at my arm.

"You shouldn't have done that. When His Majesty comes privately like this, everyone has to pretend he's not the King."

"How was I to know?" I answered her roughly. "I'm only a boy from the gutter. What should I know of courts?"

We were out in the street by now and she had put Rags down and was running to keep up with me. "What was all that about your uncle? Why didn't you tell me?"

"Why should I? Lord Maltravers is your mother's friend and he hates us. He would kill my uncle if he could."

I ran on faster, though I could hear her calling after me. "Tom, Tom, wait, please wait. Listen to me."

But I wouldn't stop. I was too humiliated, too miserable. I had dared to hope wonderful impossible things and now it was all gone and unfairly I blamed her for it. If she had not brought me here, it would never have happened.

She had reached me and pulled at my hand, but I wrenched myself free. "Leave me alone!" I shouted at her. "You're only a girl. How could you understand?"

I raced on. I knew she had stumbled to her knees on the rough road and was crying, but I didn't care. I could think only of myself. I think just then I hated her.

Chapter 8

We Make a Plan

Joshua had come back. He had called a meeting in the boys' cellar. He was perched jauntily on the barrel and we sat in a circle at his feet.

He pulled a velvet purse out of his pocket, tossing it carelessly into the air and catching it again.

"Money for expenses," he said. "Now we can really get down to business."

"Where did you get it, Josh?" asked the lame boy admiringly.

"Never you mind, Phil. One thing you can be sure of. Whoever parted company with it won't starve because of its loss."

So he had been stealing again, this time on our account. It made me feel uncomfortable. I said, "Joshua, there is some money left in the box . . ."

He cut me short. "You shut your mouth, young Tom.

This is my affair and I'll do things in my way. Now listen to me, all of you." He paused impressively. "We haven't much time. Tom's uncle is due for Tyburn on Friday week."

"Not so soon! It can't be so soon!" I couldn't stop myself, but Joshua glared at me, so I swallowed hard and he went on. "That only leaves us eight days, so we must get to work quickly."

The boys leaned forward, their eyes shining. To them it was no more than an exciting game, but I kept seeing that hateful gibbet on Tyburn Hill and the cart moving away, leaving my uncle dangling.

I realized suddenly that Joshua was still talking and I tried to stifle my fear and listen to what he said.

"So far as I've been able to find out, Tom, your uncle is the only one in the condemned cell, and as we all know, it opens out onto Press Yard. The door's a heavy one and it's locked fast, but there's a grill where the bars are set wide apart. Now, your uncle's not a big man. Let only one of those bars be shifted a trifle and he'll wriggle through easy as wink your eye."

"But they're terribly strong," I objected. "No man could move them."

"I'm coming to that. Tomorrow we slip a file to him. That gives him Friday and Saturday night to work on it. And now we come to what's really important." He stood up, looking around at the faces upturned to his, hanging on his every word. "Sunday is when the visitors flock in, dozens of 'em, men, women, and their brats, and that's when the turnkeys like to take a drink or two and spend what they've milked out of the poor wretches inside there. Fat Moll's boozing den is just inside the gate. And this is where I come in."

"What about us?" asked Rick. "What are we doing, Josh?"

"All in good time. Now I slips into Fat Moll's and with some of this good hard cash"—and he slapped the velvet purse—"I start buying drinks all round. Rogues that they are, those turnkeys will all be in like wasps round a honey jar. They'd sell their grandmothers for a free sup of brandy any day in the week."

"Am I there, Josh? Am I there?" The lame boy was jumping up and down with excitement.

"If you don't keep quiet, you'll be nowhere at all," said Joshua sternly. "Now, where was I? Ah, yes. Well, while all that's going on in Fat Moll's, you, young Phil, with Rick here, will have come up, sobbing and crying out cruel that you've come to kiss your dear dad goodbye. Once inside the cell, you hand over a bundle of women's petticoats to him. I'll contrive a signal to Tim, who'll pass it on when the coast's clear. Then he shifts the bar he's already sawn through, hops out with you two after him, and is through into the yard, with the petticoats serving to hide the chains on his ankles."

"But what about me?" I broke in. "What am I doing?"

"You're outside the gate of course, waiting for him, and as soon as he comes, you and he will make off to Ram Alley quick as your legs can carry you and there lie hid till we see how the land lies."

"There's one thing, Josh," said Rick. "What about the porter on the gate? He'll let me and Phil through, but he may stop Tom's uncle, seeing as he didn't come in with us."

"That's a point," agreed Joshua. "But there's such a fair old scrimmage and they'll never expect anyone to be walking out of that cell bold as brass and in full view of everyone. That's the trick of it, you see. It's daring to do what no one thinks possible. And Tom's uncle is not the man I think he is if he can't carry it off so the porter won't think he's anything but some poor lass coming from seeing her sweetheart and crying her eyes out under her bonnet."

That was the plot in rough outline, and to me it seemed wonderful. I didn't realize then how many things could go wrong. I passionately wanted to be the one to take the file in to my uncle, but Joshua shook his head.

"They might recognize you, Tom lad, and clap you up in the prison. Then we'd have to get you out too. All the same," he went on, "your uncle don't know any of us. We'll have to show him a token from you, or he might think it all some hoax."

"I'll write a letter," I said quickly.

"Quite the scholar, ain't we?" Joshua raised mocking eyebrows. "And where d'you think you'll find pen, ink, and paper, eh? They don't sprout on trees."

"I'll get them somehow."

"Right. Now, how to get the file to him so that no one will guess what it is."

"In a pie?" suggested Phil.

"No, it's too risky. We'd have to go to the cookshop. It would have to be too big, and greedy eyes would be on it. Some of those rascally prison-keepers might fancy it for their own dinner."

"Then how can we do it?"

"In a loaf of bread, that's how. Once the crumb is pulled out and the file pushed through the center, we can put back the crust and not a soul any the wiser. You, Gil," went on Joshua, looking down at the round dumpling of a boy, "you're the one to take it. We'll buy you a whole basket of loaves. Tidy your jacket, put on a hangdog look, and swear you've come out of charity, carrying bread to the starving poor for the love of God." Joshua spoke through his nose in the whining tone of a preacher and we couldn't help giggling at him. Sternly he went on. "Then you go round the prison handing it out, only taking good care to give the right one to Master Jeremy Hawke in the condemned cell. Now, is that clear?"

Painstakingly, Joshua went all through the plan again, so that everyone knew what they had to do, down to the last detail.

The next morning was Friday and very early I went to the scrivener on the corner of Wych Street. He sat behind a little counter with his inkhorn, his row of quills, and his sheets of paper, waiting to write for those who'd never learned to hold a pen. Love letters, duty letters, begging letters, complaining letters, bills, wills, and documents of every kind boasted the board outside his booth.

I had no intention of letting him write my letter. I put down a penny and asked boldly for a sheet of paper and the loan of a pen.

"Paper, pens! For you to blot and split!" he said testily. "Far better to let me transcribe it for you, boy!"

He was a wizened old fellow with spectacles perched on his thin nose and he leaned so far over, trying to peer around my shoulder, that it was a wonder I managed to print it out at all. Somehow I got it all set down, the bar to be filed through, the escape on Sunday, the woman's garments, all of it. When I'd done, the scrivener made a grab at it.

"Full of mistakes, I'll be bound. Let me see, boy. I'll correct them for you."

I was too quick for him. I snatched it away before he could so much as glance at it, and escaped up the street.

From somewhere or other, Joshua had got a tall hat such as the preachers wore. It was so large it came to rest on Gil's ears, and with his round rosy face pulled into a sour grimace, and speaking in a snuffling whine, he was the very image of a canting Puritan. We rolled about with laughter at him as he paraded up and down for our benefit.

Then we watched him go through the gate, and I for one could only wait with my heart leaping into my mouth. In no time it seemed he was back, grinning all over his face. We crowded around him.

"What happened?"

"Lord, they're like a pack of wolves in there. For a second I thought all was up, they made such a dead set at me, but when they would have taken all, down to the last crumb, I kept tight hold of you-know-what. I cried out in a pitiful voice that it was for a dying man and they let me go."

"How did my uncle look, Gil?"

"Pale," he said, "but cheerful. 'From Tom' I whispered when I thrust it through the bars, and he looked surprised. Then he whispered back, 'Give him my love. Tell him not to lose heart. There's still time.' "

If only I could have seen him myself, but I didn't dare to make myself known. Especially after my foolishness at the party. Maybe Lord Maltravers or the King had sent word already and they were waiting to pounce on me.

Now there was nothing to do but wait till Sunday. I saw Henry once, but she wouldn't speak to me. She stalked by with her head held high.

On Saturday afternoon I persuaded the attendant at the theater to let me creep into the topmost gallery after the play had begun, but I couldn't keep my mind on it. But then neither could the audience. They began to hiss and one of the fashionable young men sitting in the pit showed what he thought of it by buying up the entire stock of the orange girls and pelting the actors with it.

You never heard such screams. I had to laugh to see them tripping and tumbling headlong over the rolling fruit. Mistress Nell shrieked abuse, though they do say she once sold oranges herself. The actors joined in heartily, hurling the oranges back into the audience, who then fell to fighting among themselves, until the curtains drew together. I was glad Master Hart wasn't in the play that day.

At last it was Sunday. I left Rags shut up in Ram Alley and met Joshua and the boys for a final check on our arrangements. Then we set off for Newgate separately, since we felt it better not to appear with one another.

I came up to the prison from Holborn and saw Joshua talking and laughing with the porter on the gate. He had dressed himself very jauntily, with a feathered hat and a scarlet-lined cloak bought second-hand from Rag Fair, and as I watched he waved his hand merrily and disappeared inside.

As he had said, there was a great crowd of people surging in and out. Some of them were apprentices enjoying their Sunday holiday by gaping at the unfortunate prisoners. It seemed strange that only a little while ago I might have been one of them myself. A little passage led off from Press Yard. From my spot outside the gate, I could just see the door of my uncle's cell and the warder who stood outside to guard it. He looked bored and kept shifting his feet and I wondered if Uncle Jeremy had been able to loosen the bar as we had hoped.

Presently Rick and Phil came, their arms around each other, and began to plead with the porter on the gate. I drew just near enough to listen and heard the porter ask what Rick carried in the bundle under his arm.

"It's my father's best suit of clothes," sobbed Phil pitifully. "So that he may go fine to his hanging."

The man nodded sympathetically. Then he let them through and called across to the turnkey inside. I saw him unlock the iron door, and the two boys were pushed inside.

It was dreadfully hard to wait. Time simply crawled by. The sun beat down and the sweat poured off my face. The whole scheme suddenly seemed so impossible that I couldn't believe it would work. Then Gil plucked at my arm. "Look! Tim's given the signal! The coast's clear!"

Through the people going backward and forward, I could see that the guard had gone from the door, while from inside Fat Moll's bar there was shouting and laughter and I heard Joshua's voice singing some lively catch.

Strain my eyes as I would, excitement so blurred them that I couldn't see what was happening, and it was Gil who whispered, "He's through! He and the boys! Get ready. He'll be here in no time."

But then, as luck would have it, a coach came thundering down from Cheapside. It pulled up at the gate and the driver shouted for admission. The porter ran out, there was a great bustle, and the gate swung open. Once inside, two soldiers stepped out of the carriage. Between them was a tall man, his hands tied firmly behind his back, though he was handsomely dressed in a velvet coat with lace at his throat and wrists. A great mob of men and women had been following after the coach, calling out to him, and he bowed, laughing and jesting, as if he were going to his wedding instead of into prison.

"Who is it?" I asked.

"That's Swift Nicks, the highwayman," answered a woman, pushing past me for a closer look. "What a fine-looking fellow he is, to be sure."

"Highwayman?" I repeated, bewildered.

"Lord bless the boy, didn't you ever hear of Captain Hicks? He who held up a coach at dawn t'other side of London, then rode like a madman from here to York and by afternoon was playing at bowls with the Mayor and Aldermen up there, cool as a cucumber and swearing he was nowhere near Gad's Hill, where the robbery took place."

"But he's been arrested all the same," I objected.

"Aye, more's the pity, but not for that. His Majesty, God bless him, thought it a merry trick and gave him a free pardon. But he's been at his old trade again. He was always a mad, reckless fellow."

I was hardly listening to the woman's chatter. I had lost sight of my uncle and the two boys in the mob crowding around the highwayman. His arrival had caused great disturbance in the prison. The turnkeys all came running out of Fat Moll's drinking booth, and Joshua with them. He let them pass him. Like me, he searched the crowd with his eyes.

Then several things all happened at once. The Chief Warder, who had been speaking with the captain of the soldiers, issued an order. The guard of the condemned cell hurried forward to unlock it, and with a sick feeling I guessed at their intention. For safety's sake they were going to thrust the highwayman into the room and keep him locked up there out of harm's way.

The turnkey flung open the door and saw that the cell was empty. Immediately there was an outcry. In the meantime the gate had swung back to let the carriage pass out, and I caught a glimpse of my uncle struggling to force himself through the people and slip out close by the wheels.

It was foolish, but I couldn't stop myself. I called out to him, urging him to hurry, that we were waiting for him, and it drew attention to him at once. The porter began to swing the gates shut again.

Gil, Tim, and Phil came along at a rush, trying to carry Uncle Jeremy with them, but he was hampered by the woman's skirts. He stumbled, a man beside him grabbed at him, the hood of the cloak fell back, and the frilled mob cap underneath was dragged off.

"Here's your man," shouted half a dozen voices at once.

The three boys had shot through the gate just before it shut, but though my uncle fought like a madman, he could not free himself in time. The last I saw of him, he was being forced back to the cell and thrown inside to join the highwayman. The door clanged to with a horrible finality.

There was nothing we could do except get out of the neighborhood of Newgate as quickly as possible. We raced down the street, doubling down one alley and then up another before we stopped, panting.

"That danged highwayman!" exclaimed Gil breathlessly. "Just a few more minutes and we'd have done it."

I could not say anything, my heart was too full. I leaned against the wall and could have burst into tears at the failure of all my hopes.

The lame boy, who'd never been particularly friendly, sidled up close beside me as the others went on talking. "Don't worry, Tom. Josh will think of something. He's so clever."

"Clever!" I repeated bitterly and very unfairly, but I

felt too miserable to hold my tongue. "He's clever enough at stealing purses and blaming other people, but when it comes to doing something really worthwhile, all he can do is put on airs and show himself off."

"So that's what you think, young Tom, is it?" To my dismay, Joshua had come hurrying after us. He went on coolly, "That suits me. Only, the way you pointed your finger at your uncle, shouting out in front of all the world, I thought you were glad to see him recaptured."

"That's a lie! It happened so quickly . . . I didn't think . . ."

"Didn't think! That's right. Accuse everyone but yourself. You can get Master Hawke out of Newgate or let him hang as you please. It matters no more than a tinker's button to me. You go your way and we'll go ours. Come on, boys."

"Joshua, I didn't mean . . ."

But while I stood like a fool, tongue-tied, and wretched, he strode off at a great pace, Gil and Tim starting after him at once without a backward glance.

Rick hesitated. "It'll be all right," he said unhappily. "I'm sure it will. You'll see . . ." Then he grabbed Phil by the shoulder. "We'd better hurry." And they followed after the others.

The worst of it was I deserved it. No one could have guessed at the capture of the highwayman, and Joshua could have done nothing against so many. Knowing how touchy he was, why couldn't I have kept my stupid tongue still? Now I was on my own again, and the fact that it was my own fault didn't make it any easier to bear.

Chapter 9

I Go Again to Newgate

I woke up on Monday morning with the strong feeling that I must see Uncle Jeremy. I had to talk to him, I just had to, even if they put me in prison too. In fact, at that moment I don't think I would have cared if they had.

The only thing was that after all the disturbance they might not let anyone in to see him. Well, I would simply have to try, that's all.

I set out early. Rags wanted to come with me but I wouldn't let him. We were both very hungry. In all the excitement of planning the escape, I'd neglected my work at the theater. I'd gone to bed supperless. The last few coins in the black box had been spent. There was nothing but dry bread and I had nothing in my pocket. I crumbled some of the loaf for Rags, left him a bowl of water, and then I was off.

On the way to Newgate I had a brilliant idea for getting into the prison, and I was lucky. There was a different porter on the gate and I walked up boldly and asked if I might speak with Captain Hicks on very important business.

"Oh, and who might you be, eh?" asked the man, looking me up and down suspiciously. "Why should you want to see the gentleman so very urgent?"

"I'm his brother, sir," I said and managed a convincing sob. "And my poor old mother is in a terrible way, fair sobbing her heart out for him."

"Oh, she is, is she? Well, she'll be sobbin' a good deal harder before the week's out. They're wasting no time on that one. He's for Tyburn on Friday, along with that artful rogue, Hawke. Got my mate in a fine packet of trouble, he did, with his carryings-on yesterday. Come on, youngster," he went on, seizing me by the shoulders and shaking me hard, "show what's in your pockets now. Let's see how many knives, files, keys, or picklocks you've got hidden up your sleeves or in your breeches!"

He practically stripped me before he would let me through, and muttered discontentedly at my empty pockets. Then to my dismay I was marched past the cell in Press Yard, up a flight of stairs, and along a stone passage. A door was unlocked.

"In you go," said the turnkey, giving me a push and raising his voice. "Your brother to see you, Cap'n."

The highwayman in shirt and breeches was sprawled on a truckle bed. He sat up lazily.

"By God's whiskers! I thought I was me dear mother's single blessing, but it seems I was wrong." There was a humorous grin on his pleasant face. "Where did you spring from, little brother?"

The room was dark, with only one slit of a window

very high up, and I blinked at him. Now I was there I didn't know how to explain.

"I thought . . ." I began. "You see . . . yesterday . . ."

"I fear your brother is my nephew," interrupted the quiet voice I knew so well. Then I saw my uncle. He was half sitting, half lying on a bundle of straw. On one ankle there was a chain with an iron ball attached to the end of it. Another chain was fastened to a belt around his waist and firmly padlocked to a ring in the wall.

It was horrible to see my gentle, kind uncle fettered like a savage animal. I was choked with a hot, indignant rage.

He lifted up the iron ball and let it fall with a thud. "They're taking no chances this time, you see," he said with a wry smile, and I ran across to him, throwing myself into his arms.

"There, there," he said, stroking my hair soothingly. "What are a few chains, after all? They can't fetter the mind or bind the spirit. Isn't that so, Captain Hicks?"

"Never said a truer word, sir," agreed the highwayman heartily. "And is this the brave boy who would have brought off your escape last evening if I hadn't turned up like a bad penny in the beggar's bowl? My apologies, lad. Wouldn't have done such a thing for the whole world. Never felt so sorry about anything in me life."

"It was my fault," I burst out. "If I'd not called out . . . if I'd only . . ."

"No," said my uncle, "it wasn't that. I'd have escaped if I could, but fate decided against it, and no man can fight his destiny." Then he looked searchingly into my face. "Tom, who are these boys who have been helping you in this?"

"They're just friends of mine," I answered evasively, since I had a feeling that Uncle Jeremy wouldn't quite approve of the boys, or indeed of Joshua. "You see I simply had to do something or starve." I began to tell him about the theater, exaggerating a little, making what I did sound better than it was, and he listened quietly.

When I had come to an end, he sighed heavily. "It's not what I had planned. I wanted a better life for you, Tom. You would have been safely settled with Master Fox by now if this wretched ill luck had not come upon us. Now only God knows what will become of you."

"Never say die," intervened Captain Hicks cheerfully. "Not till the noose is around your neck and your legs kicking in the last dance, and even then there's hope. A young friend of mine in the same way of business as meself was cut down quick by his friends, whipped off to a surgeon and by jingo, in no time at all he was right as rain, and no man can be hanged twice for the same crime,"

"I don't think that's likely to happen to you or me," commented my uncle dryly.

"Who knows?" The highwayman waved an airy hand. "There's five days to go and a few miles between here and Tyburn. All kinds of accidents could happen. The King could die, the prison governor be accused of robbery, a coach could ram us, a wheel could fly off, the horses could take fright, and who have we in the cart with us after all —none but that mumbling old fool, the prison chaplain, and two guards, no match for two determined men with maybe a few brave friends in the crowd to lend a helping hand." And he gave me a prodigious wink.

My uncle smiled at his companion's extravagance, but though I wasn't sure whether he was serious or joking, he had set ideas seething and churning in my head. Perhaps we could contrive something. After all, there were six of us, seven if I could persuade Henry to come in with us. I felt a tremor of doubt when I remembered how Joshua had gone stalking off with the boys, but I'd get over that. I'd go back to the cellar, I'd apologize, I'd eat humble pie, anything.

The door clanked open and a rough voice said, "Come on, out of there now, young feller-me-lad, double quick!" And there was no time left.

"Goodbye, Tom," said my uncle, and pressed my hand hard. "God bless you, dear boy."

"No, it's not goodbye," I whispered fiercely to myself. This wasn't the last time. We'd save him yet.

I could hardly wait for the day to end. For some reason Joshua and the boys were not at their usual posts. I couldn't find them anywhere, and I was kept busy all afternoon running hither and thither on all kinds of errands.

And after the performance was finished and the audience had all gone home, something else happened to keep me from finding Josh. I'd just fetched a mug of ale for the doorkeeper and taken it in to him when Master Charles Hart came along the passage. He looked as splendid as any great lord and I flattened myself against the wall to let him pass. But he paused when he saw me, and put a hand on my shoulder.

"Young Tom, isn't it? Come here, boy, turn your face to the light where I can see you." He flicked my cheek lightly with his gold embroidered glove. "Not bad, not bad at all. You've the looks for it, but have you the ability, that's the point. Tell me, Tom, do you like singing?"

"Yes, sir," I mumbled, "very much."

"Enough to practice it, to learn and study and work day and night to make something of yourself, eh?"

"I don't know," I stammered. "I suppose so." I wasn't sure what he meant.

"Don't know . . . suppose so . . . that's no way to talk! Make up your mind, go right ahead, let nothing stop you, that's the way to get anywhere in this life. Has nobody taught you that lesson yet?" Impatiently he thrust me away from him. "Well, well, you're young yet, too young maybe."

He fumbled in his pocket, dropped a few coins in my hand, and went on his way to the waiting carriage.

I think at any other time the fact that he had even noticed my existence would have thrilled me beyond measure. But all I could think of at that moment was finding the boys and telling them about the plan that was bubbling in my mind.

I did look gratefully at the money in my hand. At least now I could buy myself a good meal.

I raced back to Ram Alley, fetched Rags and shared with him a splendid supper of boiled beef and pudding with buttered onions. Then with all the courage I could muster, I marched off to the boys' cellar. The door at the bottom of the steps was shut fast, but I saw a glimmer of light through the shutter, so I raised my hand and hammered on it.

There was a long wait and I banged again impatiently. Then Joshua's voice said coldly, "Who is it?"

"It's me, Tom. Let me in. I must speak with you."

"Why?" was the frosty answer, and at that I became quite desperate. "Please let me in, Joshua. I'm sorry for what I said, I am, really. I didn't mean it."

I went on pleading, and quite suddenly the door flew open and I fell into the room.

I scrambled up, looking around me, and it was almost like the first time except that Phil ran up and put his thin arms around Rags and Rick gave me a quick, shy grin.

"Where have you been?" I demanded. "I've been searching all day."

Joshua was standing unsmiling with folded arms. "We're not answerable to you. What do you want with us?" he asked coolly.

I burst out with all that had happened that morning and with what Captain Hicks had said.

"Couldn't we do it?" I went on with rising excitement. "Couldn't we stop the horses in some way? Throw pepper in their eyes, make them stampede, cause such a confusion that my uncle, and the Captain too, could escape . . ."

The boys were grinning at one another. It made me so angry that I went on still more violently, until Joshua abruptly interrupted me.

"Show him."

Gil and Rick ran to a corner and came back with a small canvas sack. They opened it and shook its contents out onto the floor. Hundreds and hundreds of glass balls, hard and round as large marbles, poured out and rolled in every direction.

I stared down at them open-mouthed and Joshua said, "Walk on them. Go on, Tom. Just try walking on them."

Then I understood. "You mean you thought of it too. We throw these down under the horses' feet as they come down Holborn Hill and their hoofs will slide and slither and then they will scream and rear as they try to regain their footing."

"That's part of it," said Joshua, "and that's why you've

not seen us today. We've been to the glassworks over at Vauxhall and begged them from the workmen. They're the throw-outs, the ones they can't sell, but it was a hard job collecting them." He smiled for the first time. "You're not the only one with ideas."

We settled down to work out our plan. Every detail had to be right, each one of us had to know exactly what he had to do, because if this failed, then Uncle Jeremy would surely hang and nothing would save him.

"We need three to throw down the glass balls," said Joshua. "It had better be Rick, Tim, and Phil. They can come from three sides at once and they must all come together just as the cart moves down the little rise from Holborn towards the Church of St. Giles."

I knew the place well. It was there that all the carts carrying prisoners to Tyburn drew to a halt and according to ancient custom a cup of ale was handed up to comfort the poor wretches on their last journey. It was there, outside the churchyard wall, that the crowds gathered, the coaches of the gentry and even the great lords sometimes lined up to watch. Once I had wanted to go myself, but my uncle had forbidden it.

"Would you gape and stare at poor unfortunates going to their death, as if they were a Punch and Judy show?" he had said.

And now he was to provide just such a spectacle himself. Just then another thought leaped into my mind. "Won't the cart already be slowing down?"

"No, because the drivers like to come down at a gallop. They take pride in reining in with a flourish," said Joshua. "I know. I've watched them many a time. And this is where I come in. There is a green alley opposite, coming out of the fields, and you and I and Gil here, who has a strong arm, will be waiting with one of the market barrows . . . I know where I can borrow one . . ."

"From Covent Garden market?" put in Phil gleefully. "Like we did before, Josh? It's easy to steal one when the porters' backs are turned."

"Shut your mouth, youngster. Borrow, I said," interrupted Joshua severely. "You know well enough Tom don't like that word steal." And he gave me a quick sideways grin. "Now, at the very moment when the horses are rearing up, we run our barrow full pelt into the side of the death cart. The whole load of fruit and vegetables will go scattering over the road, and with any luck we'll splinter a wheel. By that time, what with the horses sliding and slithering, the mob screaming and running madly after the chance of a free apple or a fine cabbage, there should be a rare old tumult. One, if not both, of the guards will be leaping down to lend the driver a hand to control the horses, leaving the prisoners roped to the cart. So then I ups with me knife, quick as lightning, and cuts them free."

"But supposing they don't both jump down?" objected Rick. "And what about the chaplain?"

"I was coming to that," said Joshua thoughtfully. "He's as fat and fearful as a scared hen, but we do need just one more to lend a hand."

"There's me," I broke in quickly.

"No, not you. Oh, you can do something, but you've got to stand ready to get Master Hawke away to Ram Alley, and if the chains have done their devilish work, he may be glad of someone to lean on. No, we do want just someone else . . ."

"There's Walt Budge," I ventured.

"Who?"

"Walt Budge. He's a boatman on the river and he's a friend of mine."

"Is he one of the babbling sort? He won't go running off to the Parish Constable with some long tale?"

"Of course he won't. He's a good man and he likes my uncle."

"Aye, well, mebbe it's a risk we'll have to take," agreed Joshua reluctantly. "If you're sure of him. But you sound him out first, cautious like, don't go giving too much away."

There was one other thing to be settled. My uncle and the highwayman had to be warned so that they would know what to expect and be ready to make the most of it, and Joshua was very firm that it should not be one of us.

"Those danged turnkeys at Newgate know us only too well," he said. "One more sight of Phil or me or Tom here and they'll suspect something is on the wing. When Captain Duval was turned off, they brought out the King's Guard, and if that happens, then where shall we be?"

There was silence for a moment, and then I said diffidently, "What about Henry?"

"Who's Henry?"

"You know . . . Mistress Gilbert's daughter."

"Oh, her!" exclaimed Tim and Gil together with a grimace.

"A girl!" Joshua was disdainful. "Full of airs and graces, she is, and fancies herself more than somewhat. We don't want none of her sort."

"She's not like that," I burst out indignantly. "She's brave and sensible, and she's fun too . . ." I broke off because I was remembering on what terms we'd parted.

Phil and Rick were dancing up and down, giggling and pointing their fingers at me. "Tom's got a sweetheart! Tom's got a sweetheart!"

"Don't be silly!" I shouted back.

"Shut up, all of you!" Joshua raised his hand for silence. "It might work. Would she do it, Tom, do you think?"

"Yes, yes, I'm sure . . ." I wasn't nearly as certain as I sounded.

"All right, but don't tell her the plan. Just ask her to take word to Master Hawke for you, and write it so it won't mean nothing, not even if those prison-keepers do happen to lay their dirty hands on it."

Between Monday night and Friday morning the days simply raced by, there was so much to be done. There were more glass balls to be collected, not only from the Vauxhall factory but from anywhere else we could beg or steal them. There were expeditions to the market to decide exactly where the barrows stood when loaded and the best and easiest route for one of them to be whisked away. We went over the ground down Holborn Hill and into St. Giles till we knew every inch and could have walked it blindfolded. I tramped to and fro between Ram Alley and Seven Dials until I was sure of the quickest way and had noted empty houses or unused yards where we could take cover if anyone came after us.

After that, I went down to the waterfront to find Walt Budge. He was friendly as ever, asking me a hundred questions as to my doings, and after I'd told him some of my adventures we talked of Uncle Jeremy.

"A bad business," he said. "A good man like Master Hawke going to his end with a rascally highway robber. It ain't decent. And the mob'll be cheering their silly heads off for Captain Hicks, I shouldn't wonder. I wouldn't put it past them to have him out of the cart and running free if they get half a chance."

"Walt," I said, "if that were to happen . . . would you do what you could to help my uncle to escape too?"

"Eh? Why?" He looked at me sharply. "What do you know, young Tom?"

"Nothing much. Only rumors, just rumors. But if it were so . . ."

"Ah, if it were so . . . then your uncle'd be a fool not to take advantage of it." Walt Budge heaved himself to his feet and clapped a hand on my shoulder. "Tell you what, lad. Don't say aught of what's going on or what's planned, I don't want to know. Just tell me where and when and I'll be there, ready and willin' . . . then we'll see what we'll see, eh?"

He was a man of his word, I was sure of that, so now only my hardest task remained. I had to find Henry. I'd not seen her for several days, though Mistress Melanie had spoken to me once very kindly as she went in at the stage door. I knew where they lived, of course, but I didn't want to go to their lodgings, so at last on Thursday morning I went in search of Master Watchet's Academy.

It was in King Street, a little distance from the theater. A tall narrow gloomy house. I could understand why Henry hated going in there. I hung about on the opposite side of the road until midday, when the door opened and a bunch of young girls came out, most of them older than Henry and all chattering like a lot of silly jackdaws. I looked at them closely as they went by, but she wasn't among them.

Several minutes later when I'd almost given up hope,

the door opened again and out she came. She had some books under her arm, and as she paused on the step, I thought she looked as if she'd been crying.

I hadn't made up my mind what I was going to say to her, but Rags settled it for both of us. He raced to meet her as she ran down the steps, and she dropped the books and was down on her knees in an instant, hugging and kissing him.

She looked up as I came across the road. "Hello, Tom."

"Hello."

She scrambled to her feet, and as she picked up her books I saw the red weals across the palms of her small hands. It had never occurred to me before that a girl could be punished like a boy. I don't know why, but I felt sorry and hotly indignant at the same time.

I said quickly, "Do they hurt?"

"Not much." Then she grinned with all her old spirit. "It was my fault, really. I told Master Watchet that I didn't need him to tell me how to speak verse because my mother was a better teacher than he could ever be, and he said, 'Pride goeth before destruction and a haughty spirit before a fall,' and that the devil of vanity had entered into me and must be driven out with the whip so that every time I moved my fingers I would remember and be sorry."

"What a horrid brute!"

"I'm afraid he doesn't like me much. He calls the theater 'a pit of iniquity,' whatever that may be." And she gave her pretty, gurgling laugh. "What have you been doing, Tom?"

"Lots of things."

She turned to look at me as we walked along side by side. "What was all that about your uncle? I did so want to ask you, and you were so nasty. It was such a muddle at the party, I don't think anyone really understood it properly, and Mistress Nell said you must have made it all up just to draw attention to yourself and that the King was quite right to be so angry."

"I hadn't made it up," I said indignantly. "It's all true, every word of it. Lord Maltravers knew that right well."

"Oh, him! I hate him."

"Why, Henry? What has he done?"

"Oh, nothing," she said quickly. "Go on, Tom, do go on about you."

"All right."

There and then I made up my mind to tell her the whole story. It didn't seem fair to involve her in it unless I did.

She listened with rapt attention. "Oh, it's wonderful," she exclaimed. "What a splendid adventure! How I would love to meet your uncle!"

"Well, you can. That is, if you'll help us and if you'll swear to say nothing to your mother or to Lord Maltravers."

"Of course I won't. Cut-my-throat-and-let-me-die before I will. Oh, Tom." She stopped still in the street. "I was feeling so miserable, and now everything's marvelous again. What do you want me to do?"

"Carry a message for us to Newgate."

"Right into the prison? Oh, goody! I've always wanted to go there and I've never been allowed even to go near it. I shall act a part. What shall it be, Tom? Shall I be a saucy serving maid, or shall I pretend to be his little sister and weep all the time?"

Henry had stopped and was already trying out voices and gestures in the open street.

"For goodness' sake!" I begged. "Do be sensible. Whatever we do, we mustn't draw attention to ourselves or let them think there's anything in the wind."

She sobered down at once. We talked it over quietly and that very afternoon in her oldest and plainest dress, with a dark shawl over her bright hair, she went with me to Newgate.

There was no doubt about it, Henry was already a splendid actress. She stood at the gate, a forlorn little figure pleading with the porter, the tears running down her cheeks and a pathetic quaver in her voice.

The man was quite obviously softened. "Five minutes only, little missy. More than that, I daren't do." And he let her go through the gates.

When she came back, she was sobbing harder than ever and it was not until we'd gone through the arch and were well away from the prison that she turned a radiant face to me, her eyes sparkling. "Didn't I do it well? They even let me go right into the cell alone, and I whispered your message while I put my arms round your uncle's neck and pretended to kiss him, in case they were watching through the spy hole. He was ever so surprised, but he said I was to tell you that whatever happened, he would never be anything but proud of you. He's nice, your Uncle Jeremy, I like him . . ." Henry paused.

"Well, go on—what else did you do?"

She blushed red as fire. "Well, you see, I had to pretend with Captain Hicks too, and put my arms round his neck, and do you know what he said?"

"What?"

" 'Tom must be congratulated on picking the prettiest messenger in all London.' Am I pretty, Tom?"

"I don't know," I said, taken aback. "I never thought about it."

"Well, he thinks so anyway." And Henry gave a little skip. "I'm coming with you tomorrow too."

"No, you're not," I exclaimed, shocked. "You mustn't come anywhere near. It might be dangerous."

"No, it's not, not for me anyway. Do you know what I'm going to do? I'm going to scream and scream, then perhaps I shall faint or have a fit. That will cause a terrible fuss, won't it?"

Nothing I could say would make the slightest difference to her, and knowing Henry, I was sure she'd do exactly what she said, however hard anyone tried to stop her. It worried me, but then, every time I thought of the next day a quiver ran right through me down to my boots, and it felt good to be friends with Henry again and know she was on our side.

Chapter 10

The Road to Tyburn

I thought the time would never pass while we were waiting for the cart to appear on top of Holborn Hill. Everything so far had gone according to plan. Rick, Tim, and Phil were at their posts. An immense crowd surged in and out of the churchyard, and I could see Walt Budge leaning against the railing, with one of his paddles casually across his shoulder as if he were on his way to work.

Among the carriages I caught a glimpse of one I knew, but my Lord Maltravers was nowhere to be seen. Only Master Nathaniel Leigh was there, in his black coat, with his crafty face, and holding a lace handkerchief against his fastidious nose.

It was the cheering that gave us the first indication. Then, as the cart came into view, we could see my uncle and Captain Hicks. Despite his hands tied behind his back, the highwayman was bowing from side to side as grand as any king, laughing and exchanging jests with some of those who ran beside the cart.

Gil grabbed my arm. "Look, Tom, soldiers!"

He was right. A trooper rode on either side of the cart.

"Damnation!" muttered Joshua under his breath, but he said nothing more and we stood tense, every nerve quivering, waiting for him to give the word.

Then suddenly the boys went into action and we were in the thick of it. At one moment we were watching the driver whip up the horses so that they came down the slope in fine spanking style, and the next instant it was a pandemonium of rolling glass balls, of sliding, slithering animals, of men cursing, women shrieking, and children screaming.

"Now!" said Joshua. "Ready!"

And we came out at full speed, ramming the barrow into the side of the cart, splintering two spokes of the wheel and sending cabbages, potatoes, turnips, apples, and the Lord knows what flying all over the cobbles.

Fortunately for us, the soldiers were desperately trying to control their plunging horses and only added to the frightful confusion. Men, women, and children had swarmed into the road picking up fruit and vegetables or chasing after glass marbles even under the horses' feet. One of the guards leaped down from the cart, cursing angrily, and I tripped him up so neatly that he fell flat on his face in the gutter.

Joshua was on the cart already, slashing at the ropes that bound my uncle and the highwayman. The chaplain had taken refuge in a corner, shaking with terror, his hands over his face. The second guard had snatched up his musket. I screamed out a warning as he raised it, but Walt Budge was before me. He brought his paddle down

with a sweeping blow that knocked the guard clean off the cart.

My uncle was beside me in the roadway now. I seized him by the arm. "This way, quickly!"

With Captain Hicks close behind us, we dived into the crowd, which opened willingly to receive us, laughing, clapping us on the back, and thrusting us forward. One of the soldiers who had dismounted and managed to quiet his horse made to follow, but Walt Budge was after him.

"No, you don't, me hearty!" he said and with the paddle caught him a whack that sent him rocking.

Then we had broken through. We were out of the churchyard and running as fast as we could toward the alleys of Seven Dials.

We had gone some considerable distance when my uncle stumbled and would have fallen if the Captain had not grasped his arm. He leaned against the wall, his breath coming in sobbing pants.

"It's no good. I'm done," he gasped. "You go on, Tom, with the Captain. Leave me."

"Nonsense, man," said the highwayman. "Take heart. You lean on me and we'll do fine."

I noticed then how pale and thin my uncle looked, and I saw the cruel lacerations on his wrists where the chains had gripped him. I had taken his other arm when I heard the pounding feet and saw at the end of the alley the black figure of Master Leigh. He must have fought his way through the crowd to follow after us.

"Quickly!" I tugged at my uncle's hand. "We must go on. We must!"

Between us we rushed him along, around one corner and down another narrow street, with the horrid fear that our pursuer was gaining on us and might well be bringing others close behind him. Somehow we had to trick him.

"In there!" exclaimed the highwayman breathlessly, and we dragged my uncle down some broken stone steps and into what we thought was a disused basement. Almost falling through the door, we went into dense clouds of thick steam and the most terrible smell imaginable. Out of it emerged a gray ghostly figure in soaked filthy rags.

"Huntin' you down, eh?" he croaked. "We don't want none of that sort in 'ere!" And he swung the door shut behind us and heaved a wooden bar across it.

My uncle sank down on a pile of sacks and I saw that the steam was rising from huge caldrons bubbling and seething on a slow-burning fire.

"What the devil are you cooking up there, my friend?" asked Captain Hicks. "It stinks worse than the pit of hell."

"Fat," answered the specter, grinning in a frightful fashion. I'd never seen anyone like him. His face was as gray as his rags, and he looked as if he'd been boiled for years in a tub and wrung out like an old dishcloth. "Fat, bones, hair, and hoofs from the slaughter yards . . . to make soap."

"Lord bless me," said the Captain, peering into the caldrons. "What a witch's brew goes to the making of a cake of soap for my lady's chamber!"

I was kneeling beside my uncle, chafing his ankles swollen and bruised by the heavy fetters.

The gray ghost slid past us, opened the door, and in a moment or two was back. "Gone past," he hissed in a hoarse whisper. "Best get goin' while you can."

"We're grateful to you . . ." began my uncle.

"No need," grimaced the soapmaker. "We ain't no friends to the law in these parts."

Already we were being thrust out and the door shut behind us.

We reached the bank of the river in safety and there Captain Hicks came to a halt.

"This is where we part company. You've saved my life, young Tom, I'll not forget that in a hurry. If ever you need help from Swift Nicks, leave word for me at the Goat in Boots. It's an alehouse on t'other side of Chelsea village." He fished in his pocket, brought out a scrap of paper, and scrawled something on it. "Show the landlord this. He'll know where to find me."

He wrung my uncle's hand and then mine and went sauntering off, whistling merrily, gay as a lark. No one would have dreamed that, scarce an hour before, he had been on his way to a horrible death.

There was so much to talk about and so much to tell, I didn't notice how weary my uncle looked or how painfully he limped as we made our way along the bank of the Thames. When we reached Ram Alley, it was to find the others had got there before us. There they all were, Rick and Gil and Tim and Phil, with Joshua and Henry and a feast to welcome us. There were pies and cakes and fruit. There was even wine, and if there'd been a penny piece paid for any part of it, then I'm a Dutchman! But I didn't care. I was too happy.

"Three cheers for Tom's uncle," shouted Rick, who had climbed onto the chest and was waving his hands above his head. "Hip . . . hip . . ." And they almost raised the roof. Then all four boys were on him, all talking at once, dragging him to the table, pushing food into his hands.

"Stop!" commanded Joshua, breaking in on the babble. "Leave him be, for goodness' sake. Let him draw breath in peace." He filled my cracked cup from the wine jug and held it out. "Here's to you, sir."

"It's I who should be drinking to you." My uncle took the wine. His eyes were on Joshua and I knew he recognized him, but he only smiled. "But for you, I'd be kicking my heels on Tyburn Hill at this very moment. My thanks to all of you." And he let his gaze go around from one to the other, till he came to Henry. Then he reached for her hand, bowed, and kissed it quite like one of King Charles's courtiers, drank down the wine with a flourish, and tossed the cup over his shoulder.

"Oh," exclaimed Henry, enraptured. "You did that beautifully. Did you see me? I screamed so much they thought I'd taken a fit, and nearly carried me off to the madhouse."

We set to work on the food with gusto, for none of us had taken a crumb that day, and though my uncle didn't eat much, he had them all spellbound with tales of the prison and the ships he'd served in and the strange countries he had seen, tales that even I hadn't heard.

Joshua sat with his eyes never leaving my uncle's face, and when Uncle Jeremy fell silent, he stirred as if waking out of a dream. "Is it so rare to sail in ships," he said, "to find new worlds?"

"It's no easy life and the company's rough, but for a homeless man it can bring its own reward." My uncle spoke quietly. His eyes held Joshua's for an instant.

Then the boy got to his feet, breaking up the party in his usual abrupt fashion. "Now, that's enough. Come on, boys. Tom wants his uncle to himself for a while."

"Oh no, Josh!" There was a chorus of protests, but he was insistent. They left reluctantly and I went with them to the door.

"Look after him," whispered Henry as she said goodbye. "He looks so tired."

I was startled by what she said. In all the excitement, I had forgotten everything except that now my uncle was free. My worries were all ended. He would look after the future. But when I turned back into the room, I saw he'd sunk down on the truckle bed and buried his face in his hands.

Alarmed, I raced across to him. "What is it? Are you sick?"

"No, it's nothing." He looked up at me and smiled in his old comforting way. "Newgate takes it out of a man, that's all. Come and sit here beside me, Tom. How long is it that I've been away? Seven . . . eight weeks?"

"It seems an age," I said.

"It is an age, and in that time you've grown up. You've surprised me, Tom. Independence, ability to think for yourself. Not in the best of company perhaps," he smiled dryly, "but who am I to judge? They've taught you a great deal, perhaps more than I could."

I didn't quite understand what he meant. "I like them," I began defensively. "It's been nice having friends."

"Of course it has, Tom. You've been alone too much." He sighed and got up, limping across to the door and looking up and down the alley before he closed it carefully, leaning back against it. "You've found yourself a fine hide-out here, but I daren't trust to it for long. They'll come searching . . ."

"The boys won't give you away."

"Of course they won't. I didn't mean that, but there are others. I can't remain shut up forever. It would be exchanging one prison for another. It'll mean moving out of the city, Tom, into the country maybe, as far away as possible."

My heart sank at the thought of not seeing Josh and the boys again, of leaving Henry and the theater. Even in all the excitement of the escape I'd not quite forgotten Charles Hart's words.

"Must we?"

I think he saw the look on my face, because he came to put a hand on my shoulder. "Well, we'll see. That's a problem that can wait for a few hours. At least until tomorrow." He stretched himself wearily. "A night's rest and I'll be a new man, Tom, fit for anything."

I persuaded him to lie down on the bed, while I made myself comfortable on a pile of straw on the floor, with an old blanket thrown over it.

After the adventures of the day, I slept soundly. Once I woke when Rags barked, and I heard my uncle stirring restlessly and muttering in his sleep. But in a moment I was fast asleep again and didn't open my eyes until a shaft of morning sun crept in at the window and went quivering and dancing across the floor.

I got up quickly, pulled on my breeches and ran to open the door. It was a lovely morning and the air that flooded in from the deserted street was fresh and sweet. Rags dashed past me, chasing one of the marauding alley cats that had dared to put its nose around our door. I laughed out of sheer happiness at what the day had in store now that Uncle Jeremy was free. Then Rags came dashing back, barking shrilly, and I hushed him, thinking my uncle was still sleeping.

When I came back into the room and went across to him, I had a shock. He was lying on his back, breathing heavily, his face flushed. His forehead, when I touched it, was burning hot and sweating. The blanket had fallen to the floor and the ankle that had borne the burden of the iron ball showed where the chain had bitten into it to the very bone.

His leg almost to the knee was horribly swollen, and when, half afraid, I put my hand on it, my uncle groaned and woke out of his uneasy sleep. For a moment he stared at me as if I were a stranger and he did not know where he was, then the wild look went from his eyes and he dragged himself up to a sitting position.

"I'm a fine fellow, skulking in bed when you are up bright and early," he said with a smile. "Give me a hand, Tom."

But, try as he would, he was quite unable to walk, and I urged him to lie down again while I fetched a bowl of water and bathed the swollen leg. The very fact that he made so little protest and lay back with closed eyes frightened me more than anything else. It was so unlike my Uncle Jeremy. I was terribly afraid that he was far more sick than he pretended.

There was a little food left over from the party, but he wouldn't eat any of it and only took a little of the wine mixed with water. At noon I thought I had better go to the theater and find out the latest news, though I didn't want to leave him.

"You run off, Tom lad. I'll be safe enough," he said cheerfully. "Rags will give warning of anyone coming near and that'll give me time to get through the back somehow and make myself scarce."

As I trudged up Drury Lane, Rick came running to meet me, bursting with excitement. "It's all over the city," he exulted. "The most daring escape for years, and they're out this very minute searching everywhere. Of course it's said to be all due to Captain Hicks, but nobody seems to have the slightest notion of how it really happened except for Josh. The soldiers described him and he's gone into hiding till the hue and cry dies down."

He sobered down when I told him about my uncle. The afternoon dragged by, and when at last the play was done, the boys came back with me to Ram Alley.

Uncle Jeremy was worse, much worse. He was obviously in frightful pain and the fever had mounted. He tossed and twisted on the narrow bed, hardly recognizing where he was. We were frantic, not knowing what to do to help him.

"I think he should have a surgeon," said Gil, looking doubtfully at the swollen leg. It had turned a deep purple and was hot and puffy under my fingers.

"But where could we find one? And even if we do, he may ask questions. Everyone knows about the escape by now."

All night we took turns watching beside him and early in the morning Phil said desperately, "I'm going to find Josh. He'll know what to do."

"No," I said. "It's no good. He's the only one the prison guards really saw. If he should be followed here, it will be all up with us. They'll find my uncle and take him back."

None of us had any thought of going to the theater that day. Rick went out foraging for food, but he wasn't very successful. He only managed to grab a loaf of bread while the baker's back was turned, and a few oranges from a market stall. We were just squeezing one of these into some water for my uncle when there came an insistent tapping at the door. We froze. Then Phil crawled across to the window and peered out.

"It's only that girl," he whispered, and a wave of relief surged through us as he unbarred the door.

Henry took one look at my uncle and turned on us. "He's terribly ill and you're all just sitting there doing nothing. Do you want him to die?"

"But what can we do?"

"He must have a doctor."

"Do you think we haven't thought of that?" I exclaimed, exasperated. "Do you think any grand physician would listen to us or come here without a shilling for his trouble? He'd have us all thrown into Newgate!"

That silenced her for an instant. Then she said indignantly, "Well, at least you could wring out some cloths in cold water and lay them on his forehead and on his leg. That's what my mother did when I had a fever." Her eyes lit up. "That's it, of course. Why didn't I think of it before? My mother . . . I'll fetch her . . . She'll know what to do for him."

"No, we can't. It's dangerous . . . I mean she might . . . No one else ought to be in the secret . . ."

I didn't know how to put my fear into words.

"Tom Hawke," burst out Henry fiercely. "If you are trying to say that my mother is a sneak and a traitor and that she would let a sick man be thrown back into prison, then I never want to speak to you again. Do you want to help your uncle, or don't you?"

"Of course I do." But I was miserably torn two ways. It would be such a relief if she were to come, but in the background of my mind was the shadow of our enemy. Whatever Henry said, Lord Maltravers did seem very close to Mistress Melanie.

The boys were waiting for me to speak. It seemed that,

with Josh not there, they all depended on me to make decisions.

"All right," I said at last. "If you're sure . . ."

"Of course I'm sure." Henry was confident. "I'll go now and I'll be back this evening."

The boys were silent when she had gone, and I felt a sudden wave of anger that it was all left to me.

"Come on," I said roughly. "Do something. Fetch some water. Soak some cloth in it."

And we set ourselves to do what Henry had told us, while we waited.

Chapter II

Mistress Melanie and My Uncle

I was sitting close beside the bed when she came in, my pretty lady in her rich silk gown, a dark cloak around her shoulders with the hood slipping back from her gold-brown hair. She looked lovely, but now she showed herself very brisk and practical. She paused only for a second in the doorway, then she came swiftly across to me. "Where is this poor man? Let me see him."

My uncle had been lying quietly. Now he stirred as I drew back. I saw her face as she bent over him, the look of astonishment and the rosy blush that ran up into her cheeks.

"Jeremy," she whispered. "Oh, my dear, it can't be you. It's not possible."

I didn't think that my uncle was conscious, but his eyes opened. "Melanie," he murmured as if in a dream. "Melanie." And he raised a hand to her cheek as if to make sure that she wouldn't vanish.

It was so unexpected that I sat there dumfounded, but the next moment it was as if it had never been, and she was crisply giving orders and had us all running hither and thither to do her bidding. Henry was carrying a basket and she began to unpack it.

Very soon the room was fragrant with the smell of sweet herbs as we boiled water and she prepared hot poultices to lay on his leg to draw away the poisoned inflammation. She worked steadily and quickly, and presently she brewed something for him to drink that smelled queer and must have been bitter, for he grimaced as she lifted his head and urged him to swallow.

She had brought sheets to lay on the bed and towels to wash and dry his face and hands. She even combed the long brown hair and tied it back with a ribbon for comfort and coolness.

Henry was watching over a pot of broth on the fire and when it was ready Mistress Melanie took it and fed him a few spoonfuls. Then she put the bowl down on the table, covering it carefully.

"Now listen to me, Tom. Your uncle should sleep very soon. I've mixed an opiate in the soup. If he wakes, give him two or three more spoonfuls, but that is all. I will try to come early in the morning before rehearsal, and Henry shall bring some food for you during the day." She looked around at the boys with a smile. "I had no notion I was to find so many willing nurses. You shall all have something to eat. I promise you that."

"It's very good of you, ma'am," I began, and asked the question that burned on my lips. "Is it all right? Will he recover?"

"I think so, Tom, I think so, with God's will."

Already my uncle looked a little easier, and when she would have moved away, he caught gropingly at her hand. "Melanie—what are you doing here?" he whispered.

"Not now," she said. "Time enough when you are well again." She slid her hand away, taking up her cloak. "Come, Henry, bring the basket. We must go."

The boys were arguing among themselves as to who should light her to her lodgings.

Smiling, she said, "I think just two of you will be enough. Now, who shall it be?" She ran her eyes over them. Phil, so small and frail, had lit his torch already. The lame boy always hated to be thought less active than the others, and I think Mistress Melanie realized it.

"This one," she said, and put a hand on his shoulder. "And one other."

"Me," said Rick, who was always quicker than anyone, and they went out together.

The next two days were strange. We forgot Uncle Jeremy was still being hunted through the city. All we could think about was saving his life, and after the first day under Mistress Melanie's care, he began very slowly to mend.

Now and again I thought how odd it was that these two should know one another, and once I even wondered about the white glove treasured so long in my uncle's sea chest, but I couldn't question him. He was not strong enough, not yet.

Then one day toward the end of the week I came in over the garden wall through the back yard and saw that my uncle was propped up against a pillow and that she was sitting on a stool close beside him. They were talking earnestly.

I heard him say, "Do you ever think of the old days, Melanie?"

It was awkward. I didn't know whether to go in or out, so I remained where I was, in the doorway.

"Of course I do," she answered him. "Often and often. It was very pleasant when we were young together in the country."

"Melanie." He leaned forward and took her hand in his. "Why wouldn't you marry me? Why did you go away as you did?"

"You know why. You hated the theater and play-acting. You said so over and over again."

"Only because I was afraid for you."

"Afraid of what? Did you think I couldn't look after myself? You knew that from a child I had set my heart on becoming an actress."

"You were promised to me. We loved each other."

"We thought we did, but it would have been useless. We would have spent our lives quarreling."

"So you went off with the players, married Christopher Gilbert and never gave me another thought." My uncle sounded unusually bitter.

"That's not true. I did think of you. Jeremy, what is the use of talking over what is past?"

Distressed, she rose to her feet, and in so doing she caught sight of me. "Look, here is Tom, come back already." She sounded relieved. "Have you heard any more news, Tom?"

"Some." I came into the room. "I've been speaking to Walt Budge. He says it's the talk of the town that the prisoners must already have escaped out of London."

"Thank goodness for that. Now they'll give up searching."

"I doubt it," said my uncle. "I must get away from this place just as soon as it is possible."

"Oh, not yet," broke in Mistress Melanie quickly. "I mean, you're not strong enough. Besides, there's Tom to be thought of."

"What about Tom? He'll come with me, of course."

"But hasn't he told you? About his singing."

"What singing?" My uncle was looking at me with a frown.

"I wasn't sure," I mumbled. "There hasn't been time."

"He has a remarkable voice, Jeremy, so sweet and true," said Mistress Melanie urgently. "I'm sure it was you who taught him, especially as he sang 'Barbara Allen.' " She looked away, a flush of color creeping into her cheeks. "It used to be our favorite in the old days. Charles was very impressed."

"Charles?"

"Charles Hart at the theater. He said Tom had a future. He asked me about him."

I stared at Mistress Melanie, hardly daring to believe my ears, but she went on hurriedly, putting a hand on my uncle's arm. "You'd not stand in his way, Jeremy. You'd not forbid it?"

"Tom, what is all this?"

My uncle's face had gone stern, but before I could reply, there came a thunderous knocking at the door.

It paralyzed us for an instant. Then Mistress Melanie said quickly, "I'll go. Tom, help your uncle through into the yard."

This was something we had planned for emergencies. I got Uncle Jeremy out into the yard, where we had made a shelter of old boxes, and went back to watch through the crack in the door.

My heart missed a beat when I saw standing on the step the black figure of Master Nathaniel Leigh.

What he said I couldn't hear, but Mistress Melanie's reply reached us clearly. "An escaped prisoner! You must be out of your mind, Master Leigh." Her silvery laugh rang out. "What should I know of such a person? I'm visiting an old servant who happens to be very sick."

He mumbled something else, and I saw how she spread her skirts, blocking his vision into the room.

"Search? My dear sir, would that be wise?" And I guessed that with one hand she was indicating the faded red cross on the doorpost. "The old woman is very ill, you know, and the doctor has not yet made up his mind as to the cause of her sickness."

"You mean . . ." His voice shook.

"How can we tell?"

When she came back a moment later, she was laughing. "I've frightened him away with a hint of the plague. He's a silly nervous creature, but all the same we might be in danger. I don't know how much he has guessed, but it is possible that he has followed me here on my Lord Maltravers's orders."

"Maltravers? What have you to do with my Lord Maltravers?"

The harshness in my uncle's voice surprised us both. He had pulled himself to his feet and stood swaying in the back doorway.

"Jeremy, you mustn't stand on that leg of yours yet!" she exclaimed. "You'll undo all the good work we've done."

She ran across to him, seizing his arm, and he let himself be helped to the bed. Then he said, "Melanie, you haven't answered my question."

"Oh, Maltravers," she replied lightly. "He haunts the theater and follows me everywhere. He likes to think he's in love with me."

"He is our worst enemy," I blurted out. "He tried to destroy my uncle. Didn't Henry tell you?"

"No, she didn't. Is this true?" She looked from me to my uncle. "But why? What should he have against you? What did you do to him?"

"Perhaps it's rather what he did to me," replied my uncle dryly. "But what does that matter? It's you I am anxious about. Don't have anything to do with this man, I beg of you. He's dangerous."

"Nonsense," she scoffed. "Do you think I can't manage a man like him?"

"You were always too headstrong," exclaimed my uncle. "If he finds out that you are linked in any way with me, he will seek to punish you too."

"How should he find out? He knows nothing of you and me."

For some reason I didn't understand, they were speaking sharply to one another. They had forgotten all about me, and I stood helpless, not knowing what to do.

"Why did he send that man of his here after you?" insisted my uncle.

She rounded on him defiantly. "Because he's jealous, that's why. He likes to know everything that I do. I tell you he is down on his knees daily, begging me to marry him."

"Marry!" My uncle laughed harshly. "You must be crazy, my dear, if you believe that."

She had picked up her cloak and flung it around her shoulders. "I am going now. I shan't come back. You don't need me any longer."

But my uncle went on, his voice hard and accusing. "Haven't you learned yet what these great lords are like? Didn't your husband die protecting you from a man like him?"

She stopped in the doorway. "Oh, how can you be so cruel! What is it to you what I do or what happens to me? If I'd known who it was when Henry told me of Tom's uncle, I would never have come here, never, never!" Her voice broke into a sob. She gathered her cloak about her and ran from the room.

"Melanie! Listen to me. I didn't mean what I said." Helplessly my uncle called to her. "Tom, go after her quickly. Bring her back."

When I got out into the alley, she had already vanished, and though I raced down to the waterfront looking for her, she was nowhere to be seen.

I went back slowly, my mind in a whirl at all I'd heard. My uncle looked up eagerly when I came in, but I shook my head. "She's gone."

"It's my fault." He leaned back wearily against his pillow. "I spoke too harshly, and she was always far too independent. Poor Tom," he went on wryly, "you look bewildered, and I'm not surprised. What has your old uncle to do with a pretty creature like Mistress Melanie, eh?"

"I heard what you said—about wanting to marry her," I confessed. "I didn't mean to listen, really I didn't."

"Well, that's long past."

"Uncle, why do you dislike the theater so much?"

"I have my reasons," he answered lightly. "And they do not need to concern us just now."

What Mistress Melanie had said had excited me. I longed to tell him about the party, about my singing and the day

Charles Hart had spoken to me, about the dream of becoming an actor, but now did not seem to be a good time. I said instead, "What did you mean about Henry's father?"

"Did she never tell you?"

"Only that he died when she was very young."

"Poor child, she must have been little more than a baby when it happened." He looked at me for a moment, then said abruptly, "It's not a pleasant story, but maybe you had better know. One of the King's dear friends, a wealthy young man who came back with him from his exile in France, began to pester Mistress Melanie with his attentions. It made her husband so angry and so jealous that one day there were high words between them and he struck Viscount Rotherham across the mouth. That was an insult no gentleman could endure from a common player." My uncle spoke with savage bitterness. "That night, as Christopher Gilbert walked back to his lodgings, he was attacked. He drew his sword and fought bravely, but they killed him."

"But who attacked him?"

"Lord Rotherham and one other. Oh, he was accused of murder. He was tried in the House of Lords by his fellow peers, but he swore he was attacked first and acted only in self-defense, so he was set free with no more than a warning. That's what I mean about the theater and stage folk, Tom. Actors are rogues and vagabonds, people of no account, whose life is not considered worth a straw. It's no life for any man, and certainly not for you."

"What did Mistress Melanie do?"

"She was very brave," he said gently. "She would accept no help from anyone. All these years she has gone on working at the theater to support herself and her little daughter—and now my Lord Maltravers threatens her. I am sure of it. He will do her harm, and we can do nothing to help her, Tom, nothing at all. If I make a single move, he will be upon me at once and it will be Newgate and Tyburn all over again."

There was something else too. Now that Master Leigh had found his way to Ram Alley, my uncle himself could be in the most deadly danger. He must move somewhere else, even though he was not yet strong enough to walk more than a few steps alone.

We talked it over and the next day, with the help of the boys, we packed up our few possessions and, with them as escort and with my arm to support him, we made our way slowly to the basement room. There we thought he would be safe till we could plan our next move, and it was there very early one morning only a few days later that Henry came hammering at the door.

I opened it and stared at her in sleepy astonishment. She looked distracted, her hair wild, her face white and blotched with tears.

"She's gone!" she sobbed. "Oh, Tom, my mother's gone!"

"Gone!" exclaimed my uncle, close behind me. "Whatever do you mean, child?"

"She never came home from the theater last night. She would never have left me alone without a word, never!" The words were tumbling out incoherently. "Something terrible has happened to her. I know it has."

She brushed past me, seizing my uncle's arm and shaking it fiercely. "Please, please, Master Hawke, you must do something. You must save her."

"Yes, yes, of course we will," said Uncle Jeremy. He put an arm comfortingly around her shoulders. "Hush now, don't weep."

His quiet tone calmed her. Her sobs lessened. The boys had come crowding around, staring and curious, but he waved them back.

"Let her be now. Come, my dear, sit down and tell us quietly what has happened."

"All right." Henry took a deep breath. "I think it all began yesterday morning."

Chapter 12

A Kidnapping

Henry's face was still tear-stained, but she told her story steadily.

"My mother was not rehearsing yesterday morning, so she slept late and she was still in her morning gown when Lord Maltravers called. She sent me down to say that she didn't want to see him, but he wouldn't listen. He went storming up the stairs and burst into our sitting room, with me behind him. 'How dare you come in here without invitation!' said my mother, but he took no notice, only spoke very roughly. 'Send the child away. I must speak with you.' My mother told me to go and get ready for school, as I was already late, but I didn't. I was afraid for her, so I sat on the stairs outside and waited."

She paused so long that I said impatiently, "Well, go on. What happened next?"

"Gently," said my uncle. "Give her time."

"I don't know what they said to one another," Henry

continued, "though it sounded as if they were quarreling. Then quite suddenly I heard my mother's voice very loud and clear. 'My life is my own,' she said, 'and it is no concern of yours whom I choose for my friends or whom I decide to marry.' 'Oh yes, it is,' shouted my lord, and he sounded very angry. 'You belong to me, do you understand? And be sure of one thing. If I can't have you, then no one else shall!' And he flung open the door and came out on the landing." Henry shivered. "His face looked absolutely wicked."

"Wicked!" I repeated.

She rounded on me fiercely. "Yes, wicked, all twisted up just like the devil in the old play. And don't you make fun of me, Tom Hawke!"

"I didn't," I began indignantly.

"Shut up, Tom," said my uncle. "Don't tease her. I know what you mean, Henry. I've seen him look like that."

She gave him a grateful look. "He went past me as if I wasn't there, and as soon as he'd gone, I ran in to my mother. She was sitting quite still. She had tears in her eyes, and I put my arms round her. But after a minute she pushed me away and asked me why I'd not gone to my dancing class. I told her it was because I feared for her, and she only smiled. 'You foolish child, what is there to be afraid of?' And she wouldn't say another word about what had happened."

The boys were sitting in a row on the floor, their eyes fixed on Henry, listening eagerly.

"What makes you think some disaster has overtaken your mother?" asked my uncle.

"Well, they were playing *The Faithful Shepherdess* at the theater, so of course she went at the usual time, because she plays the leading part. She didn't come home to

supper, but I didn't worry at first, because sometimes she sups with one of the company and they go back for an evening rehearsal. I went to bed early because I was tired, but then I woke in the middle of the night. You see, we sleep in the same room, and her bed hadn't been slept in and I knew something awful had happened to her. I just knew."

"Couldn't she have gone home after the rehearsal with one of the other actresses, with Mistress Gwynne perhaps?" questioned my uncle.

"You don't understand. She has never done that, never, never, unless she has told me first." Henry was passionate in denial. "You promised you would do something to help! You promised!"

"And so I will, but first we must be sure of our facts," replied my uncle thoughtfully. "Now, Henry, go back to your lodgings, and if there's no message for you, go to the theater and find out what you can there. Ask whether any of the actors saw her leave, whether she was alone, and which way she went. Will you do that?"

"Yes." Henry sounded doubtful. "You don't believe me, do you? You think I'm being silly."

"No, I don't, my dear, none of us do. Now, I want you to come back here at noon and tell us what you've discovered."

"But what are you going to do?"

"You will see. Will you trust me?"

Henry looked from my uncle to me and then around at the boys. "All right. I'll go."

"Good girl." My uncle patted her shoulder. "Tom, see her on her way, and then come back quickly. We've work to do."

When I returned, Uncle Jeremy said, "Now listen, all of you. I don't expect Henry to find out very much. Actors are selfish folk concerned only with themselves. If Mistress Melanie is not acting in the play today, they'll not trouble their heads about her."

"Do you really believe that Lord Maltravers has run off with Mistress Melanie?" asked Rick bluntly.

"It is possible," answered my uncle. "Perhaps she wouldn't do as he wanted, so he has kidnapped her and will hold her prisoner till she does. But where has he taken her? That is what we have to find out."

"He has a house in Covent Garden," I began.

"Yes, and another at Richmond, and a country estate in Hertfordshire," added my uncle. "And his carriage could have taken her off to any one of them."

The boys looked at one another blankly, and he ran his eye over them. "I can't command you," he said. "I'm not Joshua. I can only ask for your help."

There was silence for a moment.

"We could go and smash every one of his windows," volunteered Phil hopefully.

"I doubt if that will help very much," said my uncle, smiling, "except to earn you a sound whipping if you're caught."

Phil looked disappointed, and the boys exchanged grins. Then Rick stood up. "You tell us and we'll do it," he said. "And that goes for all of us." He looked fiercely at the others as if daring them to contradict him.

"That's what I'd hoped," said my uncle. "Now, this is what I want you to do, all four of you. Lord Maltravers has a great many servants, page boys, scullions, kitchen wenches, going in and out all the time. I want you to watch the house. Listen to their gossip, talk to them if you can, but whatever you do, don't ask too many questions. We don't want him to think he is being observed."

"Right," said Rick, who had constituted himself my uncle's lieutenant. "Come on, boys, off to your posts. What about you, Tom?"

"I'm coming," I said quickly. "You go on. I'll meet you there."

There was something I had to say first, for I remembered how often I had seen Mistress Melanie so close with my Lord Maltravers.

"Uncle," I began when they had all gone, "maybe she has gone with him of her own free will."

"No. That she would never do, I'm certain of it." My uncle sounded angry at the very notion. Then he checked himself. "And even if she had, she still would have to be stopped." He limped away from me impatiently, slapping at his lame leg. "If only I weren't tied here like this. I feel so helpless. There is something you don't know, Tom, something I should have told Melanie before she ran away from me that day." He turned to look at me. "The other man who helped Viscount Rotherham to murder her husband was my Lord Maltravers."

"Oh, it couldn't be!" I exclaimed, shocked. "Surely she must have known."

"No, she did not. His name never came out, and afterward he escaped abroad for a time. But I knew. It so happened that for a time I was engaged on work for him and I saw him go in and out that night. I heard him boast of it with his friends and that wretched creature Nathaniel Leigh, laughing at the scurvy trick they had played. It seems that he had held Christopher Gilbert in conversation while his accomplice leaped upon him from behind. It made me so angry that I forgot my place in his household and I struck out at him. He had me accused of robbery, as you know. I would have been thrown into prison there and then if I hadn't escaped, and it was then that I went to sea. It's a pretty tangle, Tom," he went on wryly, "and how we are to cut ourselves free of it, only the good Lord knows."

It certainly gave me plenty to think about as I loitered among the market stalls of Covent Garden and watched the fine house opposite with its white shutters and handsome pillared porch. It was nearly noon before my patience was rewarded. The door opened and a serving girl slipped through. Neatly dressed but not much older than myself, she tripped across the road, and I followed her in among the stalls.

She had obviously been sent to buy apricots and nectarines, for she was picking them out very daintily and arguing with the stallkeeper as I came up. I contrived to jostle her as she moved away, so that the basket jolted and half of the fruits tumbled into the gutter. I knelt to pick them up while she rated me.

"Clumsy oaf! Why don't you look where you're going?"

"Sorry, mistress. No harm done." I blew the dust off the fruit. "Can I carry your basket for you?"

"No, you can't, Master Impudence." Then she gave a little giggle. "I've only to cross the square."

"Do you live there?" I asked as casually as I could.

"Wouldn't you like to know?"

"Any chance of a boy being wanted? I could do with a job," I went on, idly kicking at stones in the gutter.

"Goodness, no! My lord doesn't employ mudlarks like you in his house." And she stuck her silly pert nose in the air.

That annoyed me, so I said nastily, "What do you do? Scrub the pots in the kitchen?"

"Well, I don't then," she replied, very haughty. "I'm in attendance on my lady."

"Oh!" That startled me. "I didn't know that my Lord Maltravers was married."

"Nor he isn't." She giggled again. "But he brought a lady home with him last evening, and a fine to-do there's been ever since, I can tell you, with me told off to wait on her. In a proper rampaging temper she was when I took her the hot chocolate this morning, fair near threw it at me."

"Fancy," I said, trying to appear unconcerned, though my heart was beating a rapid tattoo. "What was all the fuss about?"

Maddeningly, she only shrugged her shoulders. "It ain't none of my business." She shot me a sharp glance. "Nor yours neither." And before I could stop her, she had bolted across the road and back into the house.

Still, I'd found out something, and when we all met at noon and pooled our information, we had quite a clear picture of events. Henry reported that her mother had left the theater at nine-thirty and the doorkeeper had seen a carriage waiting at the end of the street as he locked up, but in a hurry to get home, he had thought nothing more about it.

Then I put in my piece, and Gil added to it. He and Tim had got talking with a stable boy leading one of the carriage horses. One of its shoes was loose, he told them, and if it went lame, his master would have the skin off his back.

"Traveling far, are you?" they asked him.

"Aye," he said. "My lord's off to the country sudden like, and the whole household too, packing up and getting ready to follow after him."

So there we were. There seemed no doubt that Mistress Melanie had been captured against her will and was being carried off to my lord's country house, and how on earth were we to stop him and get her out of his clutches? Nobody from the King downward would listen to us, a bunch of ragamuffin linkboys, and my uncle dare not so much as show himself in the streets, quite apart from reporting an abduction to the Parish Constable, without imminent danger of being clapped up and hauled off to Newgate before you could turn around.

"We must do it ourselves," said Uncle Jeremy. "Somehow we must hold up the coach, and for that we need . . ."

"Horses, pistols, and the Lord knows what else," interrupted a voice coolly. "And where do you think they're going to come from?"

Startled, we looked up. Joshua was standing in the doorway jaunty and arrogant as usual. For a moment no one moved. Then he came sauntering into the room.

"No one thought of including me in your plans, I suppose." He sounded dangerously calm.

"We thought you'd gone into hiding," blustered Gil and Rick together.

"Phil knew where I was, didn't you, Phil, eh?" And one hand shot out and tilted up the boy's white face.

"Yes, I did, Josh . . . only . . . I forgot."

"Forgot, forgot! That's a fine excuse! Jack's found a new master! Isn't that what you want to say?" There was a sneer on the thin lips, though underneath I had an idea that he was deeply hurt.

For an instant of time my uncle and he measured one another. The boys watched, their eyes traveling from the wild dark face to the quiet man in the shabby brown coat.

It was my uncle who spoke first. "You've not been forgotten, Joshua, my friend, far from it. Indeed, you came in before I could get out what was on the tip of my tongue. If our scheme was to work, there was just one person we needed, and that was . . ."

"Joshua!" chorused the boys, taking up the hint joyously.

"Surely you're not taking to highway robbery, Master Hawke, not with your top-lofty principles." Joshua was not going to give in too easily.

"Tom, tell him what has happened," commanded my uncle.

So I told him about Mistress Melanie's capture, and despite his pretended indifference, I could see him drinking in every word.

We watched him as I came to a finish. For a moment he didn't move. Then suddenly he thumped his fist on the table, his eyes alight. "By Jiminy, I'm with you. It's time someone showed his lordship that he can't do just as he likes. But there's still one other we want in this, and you know who that is . . . Swift Nicks!"

"Just the very man I had in mind," agreed my uncle. "After all, he's the professional, we're only the amateurs."

We began to work out a plan there and then.

"I'll take myself to the alehouse just off the market," said Joshua. "Some of those good-for-nothing footmen from the great houses call in there and they talk in their cups. We must know the day and hour fixed for my lord's going."

It was decided that the boys should go back to the theater for the afternoon. Too long an absence from their usual posts might cause suspicion. I was to set off at once for the Goat in Boots with an urgent message for Captain Hicks.

That left only Henry. She had been listening eagerly and was not at all pleased that there was no part for her to play in our arrangements.

"Your turn will come," said my uncle soothingly. "In the meantime, go back home and don't raise too many alarms. The less anyone talks of it, the better chance we have of succeeding."

Secrecy, an essential part of our enterprise, I almost forgot when I reached the Goat in Boots about four of the clock that afternoon. It was a little country tavern on the edge of the pretty market gardens and wooded lanes of Chelsea. There were one or two men still drinking in the taproom when I marched in and rashly asked aloud for Captain Hicks.

The landlord was a fat man with plump red cheeks that quivered like a jelly as he looked me up and down. He went on wiping his counter, deliberately ranging the pewter mugs in a neat row before he replied.

"Never 'eard of any sich captain, and not likely to, neither!" he said at last in a thick, wheezing voice. "You get out of 'ere, you young varmint, comin' in bold as brass and askin' after wretches as no honest landlord would allow to step inside his door!"

He gave me no time to protest but seized me by the collar and thrust me forcibly in front of him and out through a side entrance and into the yard. Then he released me and wagged a fat finger in my face.

"Got no more sense than a babby," he grumbled, "comin' and shoutin' out a name that could get me shut down if one of those poke-noses in there liked to turn nasty. Now, 'ow do I know that you want the Cap'n out of honesty and won't do him no injury, eh? You tell me that."

I produced the dirty scrap of paper on which the highwayman had scrawled a few words, and the innkeeper studied it doubtfully, rubbing his nose and looking from it to me before he replied.

"Ah, well, maybe that's different." He swung me around, pointing to a crazy flight of steps that led up the wall of an outbuilding. "See that there. Go on up and turn to the right at the top and you'll see what you'll see, and I don't want to know nothin', do ye understand?" With that, he turned his back on me and scurried back into the inn as fast as his stout legs would carry him.

The stairs led up to a sort of loft and there, sprawled on a great pile of sweet-scented hay, was Captain Hicks himself, sound asleep, his handsome velvet coat laid carefully over a stool, together with a gold-laced cloak and long boots of the finest Spanish leather. His pistols and his sword were lying beside him in the hay.

He was instantly awake when I breathed his name, sitting bolt upright, sword in hand. Then he recognized me and relaxed.

"Well, well, if it isn't me old friend, Master Tom, and what are you doin' here, may I ask, and how's your uncle? Still running free, I hope."

"Yes, but we do need your help most urgently."

"Ye don't say. Well, fire away, young 'un, I'm all ears.

No one shall say Swift Nicks won't lend a hand to his friends."

I gave him a brief outline of what had happened and he listened attentively.

"A wench mixed up in it, eh? Is she a pretty one? Never thought of Master Hawke as one for the ladies, but Cupid shoots his arrows where he wills." And he gave me a merry sly look. "I've had them sighin' after me too, you know, Master Tom. Now, you tell your uncle I'll be with him soon as darkness falls, and we'll concoct a plan that'll put the young lady right back into his arms and leave our fine lord high and dry like a fish on a sandbank wondering what's hit him."

I thought he was running on too fast with his talk of love and such like foolery, but that was his way, and I had his promise. That was the important thing.

There was still one more errand to be run when I got back to the cellar. My uncle had spread out our few scanty possessions on the floor and was frowning over them. He glanced up as I came in and I saw he held the white glove in his hand. He hastily rolled it up and thrust it into his pocket before he bundled the rest together again.

"Not much of value there, I'm afraid, but we must have money from somewhere, Tom." He began to tug at the ring on his little finger. He was a plainly dressed man and it was the only ornament I had ever seen him wear. He looked down at it in the palm of his hand, a heavy gold circlet with a deep blue stone. "It was my mother's and I thought never to part with it until. . . . Well, never mind. There's no help for it now, it'll have to go. Tom, take it to the goldsmith by London Bridge at the sign of the three balls. Pledge it for whatever he will let you have. It won't be much, but maybe it will suffice."

So it was that much later that evening we were all together, Joshua and the boys with my uncle and me, and on the table the little bag of silver, when a gentle tapping at the door told us that Captain Hicks had come soft-footed through the darkness.

With only a single rushlight burning and with the watchman calling, "Ten of the clock. A clear night and all's well," we gathered in a circle and plotted the rescue of Mistress Melanie and the defeat of my Lord Maltravers.

Chapter 13

We Play a New Game

Where the road to Hampstead climbs the hill to the heath, the woods grow thick and close. The trees overshadow the highway, so that even in early afternoon it is already twilight. It was there that on the following day we took up our positions.

"It's a spot with a great many advantages," explained Captain Hicks gravely. "The road is narrow, the horses will be laboring as they come up the hill, and the coachman will be far too anxious about getting his carriage to the top to keep a close watch."

So there we all were, down to little Phil, since not one of us was willing to miss the smallest chance of adding his own contribution to the night's work.

As a matter of fact, we all had our allotted tasks. As soon as Joshua brought back the information extracted from one of my lord's servants, the highwayman had sat down to work out a plan.

Horses were essential, of course. He had his own chestnut mare, but Joshua hired one for himself and one for Uncle Jeremy. Captain Hicks provided pistols and at my uncle's request procured an extra sword. He handed it over with a grim smile.

"Take care, my friend, my lord has a dangerous reputation where swordplay is concerned."

My uncle said nothing, contenting himself with drawing the sword out of its sheath and weighing it for a moment in his hand before he buckled on the sword belt. It seemed that there was always something unexpected to discover about him, and he did look splendid with his coat well brushed, a hat with a gold band, and a fine plush cloak of a deep mulberry color which Henry brought and would not say where she had got it.

My uncle swirled it around him. "How do I look?" he asked, smiling. "Fine as one of your play actors, eh?"

Henry clapped her hands, and I guessed it had come out of the theater wardrobe, but I said nothing. After all, she couldn't come with us, so it wasn't fair to make fun of her.

We each made our way to our meeting place, and I must say, when Captain Hicks assembled us in a little clearing of the wood, I thought we looked a brave sight, and my heart was beating high with excitement.

The highwayman issued his last instructions crisply. He and my uncle and Joshua had tied black silk handkerchiefs around their faces, so that only their eyes glittered beneath the curving brims of their hats. Then they withdrew into the trees and the boys and I found hiding places behind the bushes—Rick and Gil on one side; Tim, Phil, and I on the other.

One of our tasks was simply to make so much noise and cause so much confusion that the two footmen riding at the back of the carriage would think us a much larger force than we were in reality.

"More than likely they'll drop their muskets and run like scared mice at the first squeak," said the Captain contemptuously.

The waiting was the worst. According to Joshua's informant, my lord was to have set out in early afternoon, but the time dragged by and still he did not come.

It was a lonely road and there were very few travelers. The day had been sultry, a prickly sweating heat, and to make matters worse, the bed of dry leaves on which Phil and I were sitting was infested with a regular army of ants. Very soon we were nearly crazy, scratching at ourselves. They got into our breeches, up our sleeves and down our necks, and no amount of shaking would dislodge them. Tim rolled about with laughter at our antics as we tried to get rid of them.

It must have been past six of the clock when we heard the unmistakable sound of wheels crunching on the road and, peering out, I saw the horses and, beyond them, the gold and scarlet of my lord's carriage. As they drew abreast of us, I noticed the coachman had a man seated beside him. Then, as we watched breathless, our hearts in our mouths, we saw the three horsemen ride out across the road, their pistols leveled, Captain Hicks slightly in front.

His voice rang out clear and threatening. "Stand, my friends. Pull up your horses. We have you covered. One move, one shot, and you're dead men!"

The carriage lurched to a halt on the crest of the hill. The man beside the driver raised the musket across his knees, but again the highwayman's voice checked him. "One move, I said, and we blow out your brains! Watch them, gentlemen."

The two footmen had leaped down from the steps at the back, and that was our cue. With bloodcurdling yells we came out of the thicket, all five of us, in such a rush that they were taken by surprise. And this was where Joshua's brilliant notion came into force. Gil and Rick carried between them a big stretch of corded netting such as the fishermen use on the Thames. They cast it over the two men before they realized where the assault was coming from. Helplessly entangled, they thrashed about, cursing and trying to fight their way out, but we had them firmly pinioned, and the Captain was right. They were not going to risk too much injury for their master's sake.

By now my lord had let down the glass of the window and thrust out his head. "What the devil is going on? Will! Ben! Where are you? Get rid of these rascals!"

"Not so fast, sir, not so fast."

Captain Hicks, still with his pistol leveled, rode up to the side of the carriage.

"Thieving rogue!" exclaimed Lord Maltravers. "Nat, d'ye hear me? Throw this cutthroat my purse and let us drive on!"

It was then I realized that Master Leigh was the man sitting beside the coachman.

"Oh no, my lord," went on the highwayman, his tone merry and confident behind the black mask. "It's not your money we want, nor your watch, nor your jewels, but the lady." And he leaped down from his horse and swung open the door, letting down the steps and standing aside with a courtly bow. "Deliver Mistress Gilbert into our hands and you can go free as air, sir, you and your henchmen with you."

"Never, never! You saucy malapert!" shouted my lord in fury.

I think Mistress Melanie must have been struggling with him in the coach, for she cried out, "Let me go, let me go!" And the next moment she was stumbling down the steps and would have fallen if Captain Hicks had not put out an arm to support her.

Lord Maltravers followed her. He seized her roughly, dragging her away from the highwayman and thrusting her behind him. Then he drew his sword, backing up against the carriage.

"Come one step nearer and I'll kill you, you insolent wretch. I'll kill anyone who would take her from me."

"Is that so?"

My uncle had come forward. He had dismounted and left Joshua with the two pistols leveled at Leigh and the coachman. They made little protest and I knew that they, too, were not at all willing to lose their lives to serve their master's whim.

Uncle Jeremy had come closer, still masked. The embroidered cloak flung around him and the hat with its mulberry feather were clearly visible in the fading light.

"Chris Gilbert! It can't be! It's not possible!"

The look on my lord's face was one of pure terror and now I suspected that Henry had deliberately brought her father's clothes.

"No, not Chris Gilbert," said my uncle, throwing aside the hat and tearing off the mask. "Not the man you helped to murder but his friend and his wife's friend. Let Melanie go free and I swear there's an end of it."

But Lord Maltravers had recovered himself. "So that's it. I was right. It is you who've come between us," he said with ringing contempt. "You, Jeremy Hawke, one of my servants, a jailbird turned highway robber. You'll be hanged for this twice over, my man, d'you hear?"

"Maybe," replied my uncle coolly. "But if I am, then I'll take you with me." And he drew his sword and launched himself at his enemy.

"This is madness," exclaimed Captain Hicks. "Have you gone out of your mind?"

"Stand aside," shouted my uncle. "This is my affair."

I think luck, desperation, and a fierce hatred must have fought on Uncle Jeremy's side, for there was no doubt that my lord was an accomplished swordsman and, in addition, he was not hampered by a lame leg.

I could not take my eyes off them, though my breath choked in my throat and at any moment I expected to see my uncle fall with the sword thrust through his heart. I think Mistress Melanie thought so too. She was huddled against the carriage, still as a statue, hardly drawing breath, her hand pressed against her mouth.

The end came suddenly. My lord was perhaps too scornful of the man with whom he was fighting. He made so vicious a lunge that it brought a long whistle from the Captain, but somehow my uncle parried it and then he seemed almost to leap at his opponent.

The road was rough and stony and my lord was wearing light shoes, not heavy riding boots. The heel must have turned over. He stumbled backward, the weapon flew out of his hand, and my uncle was on top of him, sword poised at his throat.

"Don't kill him! Jeremy, don't! You must not!"

Mistress Melanie had sprung forward. She was tugging

at my uncle's left arm and he gave her one swift glance.

"Why?" he said with bitterness. "Does he mean so much to you, your husband's murderer?"

"No." There was a sob in her voice. "No, I hate him. It's you, Jeremy, you, don't you understand? If you kill him, nothing and no one, not even the King himself, can save you."

My uncle paused a moment, then he stepped back. "Get up," he said curtly, and resheathed his sword.

I don't think I ever saw so much concentrated hatred in anyone's face as there was on Lord Maltraver's as he scrambled to his feet. I think he would rather have died than been granted his life by a man he despised. Up on the box, Master Leigh had a sneer on his face, the two footmen, whom we still held tied down, were grinning, and even the coachman had a look of surprised contempt.

"Your carriage waits, my lord," said Captain Hicks with a mock bow, holding out the fallen sword.

It was the last touch to my lord's humiliation. Maltravers snatched the blade, snapped it across his knee, and cast it aside. Then he glared around at us, his voice thick. "You'll pay for this, every man jack of you. If there's any justice left in the King, you'll pay for this!"

He climbed back into the carriage. Captain Hicks slammed the door shut and shouted "Drive on!"

The coachman whipped up his horses and very slowly the carriage jerked forward.

We stared after it. We had won a victory, but somehow it didn't feel like one.

Mistress Melanie was looking from one to the other of us. "How can I thank you," she murmured. "I felt so alone. When the carriage was stopped, I didn't know what to think, and now . . ." She broke off tremulously.

Captain Hicks took both her hands in his, lifting them gallantly to his lips. "Delighted to have had the privilege, ma'am. Never enjoyed anything so much in me life."

"You have all been so good to me," she went on, "all of you. Tom, dear Tom. . . ." And she put her arms around me and kissed my cheek. ". . . And the boys too." She knelt down and hugged Phil. Only to my uncle she said nothing, and I thought she was very near to bursting into tears.

He stood at one side watching her. Then he said abruptly, "The sooner we get you home, the better."

"You're dashed right there," agreed the Captain. "Pity you didn't finish that one off, my friend. The only good snake is a dead one. If I'm not mistaken, he'll have the hue and cry out after us, and that before the night's many hours older."

"Aye," said my uncle. "We'd better get away separately. I'll take Mistress Gilbert up behind me and, Joshua, you'd best carry young Phil. He looks ready to drop. As for the rest—"

"Don't you worry about us," I broke in. "We'll find our own way back."

"That's right," said Rick sturdily. "We'll go just as we came, and we'll all meet tonight at the usual place."

And so it was arranged. I watched my uncle ride slowly down the lane with Mistress Melanie behind him, her arms around his waist. I didn't see him again until very late that night, when we'd eaten our scanty supper and I was lying in my own particular corner, all the stirring events of the day so jumbled together in my mind that sleep was miles away.

I heard the door creak, Rags whimpered, and I saw my

uncle slip soft-footed into the room. Presently he came over and slid under the blanket beside me.

"Tom," he whispered after a moment. "Tom, are you awake?"

"Yes. Was everything all right? Is Mistress Melanie safe?"

"Quite safe."

"Why are you so late?"

"Since I left her with Henry at their lodgings, I've been walking and thinking. Tom, listen to me. As things are, I shall always be in danger. Lord Maltravers will never forgive me for tonight's work, and he will look for revenge. It would be best if I were to go back to the sea. There, no questions are asked, and this time you shall go with me."

"No! I don't want to!" The protest burst out of me before I could stop myself.

"Why, what's this? You used to say you'd like it above all things."

"But that was a long time ago, when I was little . . . before . . ."

"Before you had your head filled with this play-acting nonsense, and before you got in with this company, is that it? Oh, they're fine lads, I'm grateful to them and always shall be till my dying day, but they're not for you, Tom lad. Do you want to be like Captain Hicks, like Joshua, living always in hiding, driven from gutter to gutter?"

"No, but . . ." I didn't know how to say what I felt.

My uncle was silent for a moment before he went on. "Tom, do you remember your father?"

"Not very well. Not now."

"He was an actor, and it was the death of him. It had

always been a hard life, and he had no means to take you and your mother out of London when the pestilence came, and so they died, as you might well have too."

My father—I had never dreamed of such a thing. It was like a revelation. It strengthened my purpose. It gave me courage.

"But that was years and years ago. Why shouldn't I do as he did? Perhaps that is what he would have wanted, and Master Hart did speak to me. You remember what Mistress Melanie said."

"Never mind what she said." My uncle sounded unusually harsh. "It is nothing to do with us. It is I who decide what is best for you."

"But I thought—"

What had I thought? That now it would be different. That now they must come together, perhaps even marry—it had crossed my mind. I knew how much they liked each other.

"Well, what did you think?"

"Nothing," I mumbled. I couldn't say what I thought. He would only be angry and it would do no good.

"Very well, then. Go to sleep now. We'll talk of this again in the morning."

He turned his back on me, pretending to sleep, but I was wide awake. My uncle's escape, his illness, and now the rescue of Mistress Melanie had so filled the last weeks, there'd been no time to think about myself, but inside me something had been growing and changing. I didn't want to leave Henry and the boys and above all the theater, yet how could I let my uncle go away alone? I was all he had, and without him I wouldn't even have been alive. It was a problem to which I had no answer.

Chapter 14

The King Plays a Part

It so happened that we never had that talk, for very early next morning there came such a hammering at the door that we started up in alarm, staring at one another.

"Open in the King's name!" thundered a voice, and the knocking on the door came louder than before.

The boys were sitting up. I scrambled to my feet, reaching for my breeches.

"Run quickly," I said to my uncle. "You can get out at the back. I'll keep them as long as I can."

But he didn't move. "No, Tom," he said. "Let them in."

Joshua said, "Don't be a fool. Go quickly."

The boys were huddled together, watching us with frightened eyes.

"They'll take you back to the prison," I urged.

"Tom," said my uncle, quite calm, "go on now. Do as I say."

Reluctantly, I unbarred the door. Outside on the step

stood a sergeant of the King's Guard, and behind him I could see two more troopers waiting.

"Master Jeremy Hawke!" he asked.

"I am here." My uncle came forward. "What do you want with me?"

"I must ask you to accompany me if you please. His Majesty's express command, and the boy too. If this lad here is your nephew?" And he stared down at me hard.

"Yes, this is Tom. Have we leave to dress ourselves?"

"Aye, but make haste about it," said the officer. He and the two men came into the room, looking around grimly while we scrambled into our clothes.

When we were ready, Rags begged to come with me, but my uncle shook his head and I had to put him back inside. Phil grabbed him and I had a sick fear that I might never see him or the boys again.

"Come, Tom," said my uncle quietly. "We mustn't keep the gentlemen waiting."

To my intense surprise, we weren't marched off to Newgate but down to the water's edge, where a boat was waiting. We stepped in, the soldiers followed us, the boatman bent to his oars, and we shot down the river toward Westminster.

"Where are you taking us?" My uncle was frowning. "Surely this is the palace of Whitehall."

"Aye, so it is," said the sergeant shortly as the boat drew in to the shore. "Mind those steps now. That green slime is slippery."

More and more bewildered, we were hustled across the strand to a small private door in the palace wall. It was opened at once to the sergeant's knock. We went up a flight of stairs, along a corridor dimly lit by high windows, to another door, where we halted while the soldier tapped respectfully.

It was unlocked by the fair man I had seen at the party. He looked us over carefully and then nodded to the guard. "That will do, Bates. You wait here with your men for further orders." He turned to us. "Follow me."

A further stone corridor, the floor thick with rush matting, and still another door, this time hung with a rich tapestry.

Our guide rapped very gently. There was a murmur within and he swung open the door.

"Master Jeremy Hawke, Your Majesty, and the boy."

I still didn't believe it. It couldn't be true. It must be a dream and at any moment I would wake up with Rags licking my face.

It was a small room, sparely furnished except that around the walls were ranged tables and chests crammed with fascinating objects, clocks of every shape and size, ornaments in gold and silver, mathematical instruments, a brass sextant and astrolabe that I knew from my uncle were used at sea, models of ships, and at the far end, bent over an odd-shaped tube, stood the King himself.

He looked up as we stood hesitating in the doorway. "Ah, there you are." A keen glance from the shrewd dark eyes swept over us. "Come in, come in. Chiffinch, is my Lord Maltravers in the presence chamber?"

"Yes, sir. He's been there some time, very agitated and demanding to speak with Your Majesty."

"Very well. Fetch him here."

Chiffinch bowed and withdrew, closing the door. We stood silent, not daring to utter a word, and the King went back to his instrument.

"Come here, boy," he said abruptly after a moment. "I want to show you something."

"Go on," whispered my uncle as I stood dumb, and he gave me a push.

I went forward slowly. A small spaniel had emerged from under the table and stood in my path, regarding me with bright brown eyes.

"Come along, come along. Surely you're not afraid of Bijou," said the King impatiently. "Have you ever seen a microscope before? No, I think not. Now, look through that and tell me what you see."

I peered cautiously through the long tube on its brass stand and at first in a flutter of agitation could see nothing at all. Then my vision cleared and I started. I was looking down at a ferocious monster crawling across a white desert, a monster with a great jaw that opened and shut, with two legs which twisted and rubbed against one another, waving horribly in the air.

"It's beastly," I exclaimed and drew back. "What is it?"

The King laughed. "It's a fly, just a common little house fly caught in a box. See?"

I stared at it and then at him.

"It's like magic."

"No, not magic, Tom. Just glass ground so cleverly by Master Robert Hooke that, when one piece is set against another, they magnify a hundred times, creating a whole marvelous world of minute objects that we never knew existed."

It was so extraordinary that I quite forgot where I was and in whose presence I stood. I said eagerly, "Please, may I look again?"

Just then the door swung open and, without even waiting to be announced, my Lord Maltravers came storming into the room. "I have been waiting and waiting, Your Majesty, since early this morning," he began at once, but checked when he saw my uncle and me. "What are these wretches doing here?"

"That surely is for me to say," replied the King coldly. He had changed again. He didn't look genial or smiling any longer. He seated himself on the only chair in the room and threw a stern glance from my uncle to Lord Maltravers.

"Your complaint was laid before me late last night, but there are two sides to every question, my lord, and I prefer to sift this matter for myself. Abducting one of the young ladies from my theater is a very serious offense, but then so is dueling and so is attempting to murder one of my subjects." And the dark eyes turned on my uncle. "What have you to say to that, Master Hawke?"

"Surely you will not listen to this liar, this thieving rogue, this jailbird." Lord Maltravers was stuttering with rage.

"I would listen to him if he were a stinking beggar from a leper house if necessary," replied the King coolly. "Please proceed, Master Hawke."

Very briefly and in his own calm, quiet way, my uncle sketched in everything that had happened, his escape from Newgate, his illness, Mistress Melanie's care of him, the night of her rescue, only leaving out any reference to Captain Hicks or Joshua and the boys.

The King listened intently, not a muscle moving in the dark face.

"It would seem that I have a couple of desperadoes for subjects, you and your nephew between you," he remarked at the end. "As a matter of interest, Master Hawke, why didn't you kill him when you had him at your mercy?"

"Because my uncle is a good man, he would not do murder," I blurted out, "and because Mistress Melanie pleaded for him."

"Lies, lies, nothing but lies," cried out my lord.

"I don't think so. It sounded remarkably like truth to me." I swear I could see the King's lips twitching, but his voice remained grave. "It's a mighty fine scene for a play, wouldn't you agree? You on your back in the dust and gravel of the road with your rival's swordpoint at your throat and a pretty woman begging for your life?"

"I'll not let this man live," screamed my lord in a frenzy. "I'll not be the laughingstock of the town."

"I'm afraid it's too late for that," commented the King. "It's too good a story, and you had too many witnesses. You should think before you indulge in such crazy frolics, my friend. You had better take yourself off into the country for a while. Let it die down."

"Is Your Majesty banishing me from the court? Is this the King's justice?"

"It happens to be my justice, and you can consider yourself fortunate," said the King, suddenly stern. "If I remember rightly, this is not the first time you have been linked with an outrage of this kind. My patience is wearing thin. You will make your preparations to leave at once, if you please."

For one moment Lord Maltravers looked as if he would have argued, but then he turned and flung out of the room.

"Well, now." The King was looking at us. "What am I to do with you, eh?"

My uncle did not move. He was standing very still and proud, his head held high. I knew nothing would induce him to plead for himself. He would die first, so it had to be me.

I fell on my knees. "He is innocent, Your Majesty," I began. "He has done nothing. It was all a plot . . . he—"

"Get up, get up," interrupted the King. "I heard all this once before, and it grows tedious. If I set your uncle free, it will be for one purpose only, and that is to keep you in better order, young Tom. I really cannot have a mob of rebel children upsetting my prison-keepers, seriously damaging my horses, and causing public riot and confusion. Do you understand me, Master Hawke?"

"Very well, sir."

For the first time, my uncle's calm was disturbed.

"Good. I know a little more of you than you think. Did you not address an appeal for help to the Navy Office?"

"Yes, I did, but—"

"How did I know that? Well, it so happens that Master Pepys discovered it only last night. It seems your letter had been buried beneath a mass of other matters while he was away at the dockyards. He brought it to me at once."

My uncle put his arm around my shoulders. "We are deeply grateful to you, sir, both Tom and I," he said huskily.

"Well, prove it in future," said the King, dismissing us with a wave of his hand. "And I've one other piece of advice for you. Marry the girl. That will put a stop to nonsense of this kind."

He stretched out his hand and we kissed the white fingers. Then we were outside and Chiffinch was hurrying us along the passages and out of the door.

But if you think that all our troubles were ended and

we'd now live happily ever after, then you don't know my Uncle Jeremy. He was a proud man, and whatever the King might say and however much he was drawn to Mistress Melanie, she was a very successful actress and he had nothing. We were beggars, both of us, and he was not prepared to accept charity from anyone.

When we got back to the cellar, it was empty except for Rags. My uncle said, "Come on, Tom, pack up our possessions. We'll go back to Ram Alley."

"Can't I go and tell Henry and the boys?" I asked. "Please, uncle. They will be wondering what has happened after this morning."

"Yes, I suppose they will. We do owe it to them after all." My uncle smiled ruefully. "Truth is it's all been so unexpected, I scarcely believe in it myself. But don't be late back, Tom. After what the King said, I'm going to find out what is happening at the Navy Office. I may have good news for you."

My heart sank, for I knew what that could mean, but I nodded and hurried off as quickly as I could to Mistress Melanie's lodgings. I saw Henry first, and she was so excited by what I told her that she flung her arms around my neck and hugged me. Then we raced each other up the stairs and burst into her mother's sitting room, both talking at once.

"Stop, stop!" she cried, putting her hands over her ears. "One at a time, please. Now you, Tom, what is all this about the King?"

"I still don't see how he could have known so much about us," I said when I had told her all about that amazing morning.

Mistress Melanie smiled. "His Majesty has eyes and ears everywhere. He never seems to notice what's going on, and yet nothing ever escapes him, or that's what Mistress Nell says about him, anyway. Why didn't your uncle come with you, Tom? I would have liked to thank him properly for all he has done for me."

"He wants to go away," I said wretchedly. "We're to go to sea, both of us, for months and months, maybe years."

"But why?" broke in Henry. "Whatever for? It seems so silly now. I thought he—"

"Hush, child," interrupted her mother. "Master Hawke must do what he thinks right, and he is Tom's guardian. It is for him to decide what is best for his nephew. I tell you what, Tom—" And she turned to me, her eyes very bright. "We'll have a party to celebrate. Would you like that? We'll have it at Ram Alley for the boys, for Joshua and Captain Hicks, everyone. I'll see to the food and you shall carry the invitation to them."

She was as good as her word, so that when my uncle came back that evening it was to find us all exceedingly merry. It was late and we had started without him. The table was loaded with food, Joshua and the boys were there, and presiding at the head was Mistress Melanie, dressed in rosy satin and looking as grand as if she were supping with the King himself. Beside her was Captain Hicks, excessively handsome in his fine velvet coat with ruffles and ribbons and laces.

Uncle Jeremy stood for a moment in the doorway, taken aback at the transformation of the room, the candle-light, the crowded table, and the gay company around it.

"The conquering hero himself," exclaimed Captain Hicks, leaping to his feet. "Come, sir, take the place of honor at your own festive board." And ceremoniously he handed my uncle to a place on the other side of Mistress Melanie.

"Is this your doing?" I heard him whisper as he sat down.

"Yes, why not?" she replied coolly. "I wanted to show the boys my gratitude."

It was a great deal later that Captain Hicks called for a song and the boys all shouted for me. I fetched the lute and pushed it into my uncle's hands. He laughed and began to play the air that had been sung all through the Fleet in the time of the Dutch wars.

We trolled out the chorus all together, beating with our fists on the table.

> "*Then if we write not by each post,*
> *Think not we are unkind;*
> *Nor yet conclude our ships are lost*
> *By Dutchman or by wind.*
> *With a fa, la, la, la, la* . . ."

Afterward, while he was still plucking idly at the strings, Mistress Melanie said, "What are you going to do?"

"The *Swiftsure* sails for Tangier in a week. I can sail as clerk of the accounts, and Tom can go with me."

"Why must you go away? Jeremy, why?" she went on. "You were employed here once before, why not again?"

"I cannot stay here, not now. There is no room in your life for me, my dear. You know that. Tom and I, we belong to another world."

"Oh, you fool," she said very softly. "You fool!"

Then suddenly she stood up, clapping her hands for

silence. "Tom, will you do something to please me? Will you sing 'Barbara Allen'?"

I couldn't think why she wanted it, because it's such a sad song. I like the melody, but it's all about a girl who's so cruel to her lover that he dies, and then she finds out too late that she loved him after all and she dies too.

"Must I?" I muttered rebelliously.

"Yes, you must," said Henry, and pinched me so hard that I nearly cried out. "I'll play for him. May I?" she went on, and my uncle let her take the lute from him. It was then that I saw he must have redeemed the ring, for he was wearing it again on his little finger.

Everyone fell very silent and I had almost reached the end of the ballad when I realized that Mistress Melanie was singing the lines with me.

> "*A cruel creature that I was*
> *To slight him that loved me dearly,*
> *I wish I had been a kinder maid*
> *The time that he was near me . . .*"

There were tears in her eyes and I saw my uncle turn to her with a look on his face that I had never seen before. It so surprised me that I stopped singing.

"Go on," hissed Henry under her breath. "Don't stop now, for goodness' sake!"

I got through the last verse and under cover of the clapping I murmured, "Did you see?"

"Yes, I did," she whispered back. "What an age they've taken over it, but I knew my mother would win in the end."

"Do you mean—?"

"Look."

Mistress Melanie had taken my uncle's hand and after a moment I saw him draw off the ring and put it on one of her fingers. She held it against her cheek for a moment, smiling.

"Thank heaven that's settled," said Henry with a sigh of relief. "Now you won't have to go away."

And she was right, because now we are all together. They were married very quietly, and my uncle is back at the Navy Office. I am taking lessons with a singing master and Charles Hart has been very kind, but I am going to have to hurry to catch up with Henry. She is to play her first part at the King's Theatre very soon now.

It was Joshua who sailed with Rick in the *Swiftsure*, and Phil practically lives with us and Rags. As for Gil and Tim, Uncle Jeremy says there are openings for clever boys everywhere.

It has been a wonderful adventure, and it was Captain Hicks who said, "It all goes to show that you must never despair. Things can come right even at the very last moment, as the hanged man said when the rope broke! You set it all down, me boy."

So that is what I did, and here it is.

Historical Note

The Link Boys is fiction, but it is based on an authentic background. In seventeenth-century London there was no street lighting except for the occasional lantern set up by a wealthy shopkeeper or careful citizen outside his house, and the boys with the "links," the old name for torches, were in constant demand. These boys were recruited from the poor and the homeless, the waifs and strays of the city with none to care for them. They waited outside public places or at street corners, earning a meager living by lighting those people who were out after dark along the rough, cobbled roads to their houses.

At this time the penal laws in England were very severe. Men and women could be hanged for stealing anything worth more than a shilling (about ten shillings, or one and a quarter dollars, in present values). Conditions in Newgate as in the other prisons were appalling except for those who could afford to pay for comfort. But discipline would appear to have been slack, and a great number of prisoners escaped. Jack Shepherd, some years later than my story, escaped three times from Newgate, despite being heavily fettered. On the third occasion he had been confined in a cell within the very heart of the prison.

Escapes on the road to the gallows were also frequent, particularly among the highwaymen, the idols of the populace. There were also one or two instances in which the victim was cut down by his friends before the customary fifteen minutes on the gibbet had expired. He was then rushed to a surgeon and his life saved.

"Swift Nicks" is a historical personage. His ride to York is the reality behind the legend of Dick Turpin and his famous horse. Charles was so amused by his exploit that he had him brought before him at Whitehall, gave him a free pardon, and bestowed the nickname "Swift Nicks" on him. He seems to have been in the same gallant tradition as Captain Claud Duval, a Frenchman who once held up a lady on Hampstead Heath and, though she had £400 in her possession, took only £100, provided she danced a coranto with him on the grass in the moonlight.

There are many instances in which Charles intervened in minor matters, tempering justice with mercy. His apparently careless manner concealed a shrewd observation and an intimate knowledge of everything that went on, a trait which sometimes disconcerted his courtiers. He could therefore have very well played a part in Tom's story and saved them from the anger of the unpleasant Lord Maltravers. His attendance at private parties incognito in the early years of his reign was the despair of his attendants, who feared attack or assassination. The "cabinet," or small room where he kept his "treasures," was in his private apartments at Whitehall, and he was in the habit of showing them to those he favored and at the same time conducting there business he wished to keep private from the curious eyes and ears of the court.

The violence of some of the younger courtiers was notorious, and an actor's life could be precarious. Mistress Melanie's story is based on an actual case. William Mountford, the young leading actor in Thomas Betterton's company, was murdered on his way home by a certain Captain Hill, who was jealous of the favor shown him by one of the actresses. His friend, Lord Mohun, engaged the actor in conversation while the captain attacked him from behind. Mountford defended himself but was seriously wounded and died the next day. Captain Hill escaped abroad. Lord Mohun was tried for murder by his peers and acquitted. Some years later this nobleman fought a duel with the Duke of Hamilton in which they were both killed.

The air "Barbara Allen" was a great favorite in Restoration times and Pepys used to enjoy hearing it sung by the pretty actress, Mistress Knep. The spirited ballad sung through the Fleet was written by Charles Sackville, Lord Buckhurst, later Earl of Dorset, on the eve of the great naval battle fought with the Dutch on June 3, 1665, in which he played a gallant part.